Comics, Cons & Clerics
J.M. Guilfoyle

Nerdy Mom Writes Press

Contents

Chapter One

Applesauce

Rina

"Oh, my god! I'm so sorry!" A guy squealed at me as an entire large latte crushed between us.

Which just so happened to leave me with pale brown dripping down my cream blouse and soaking into my pale jeans. Somehow, the dude who rammed me ended up with nothing on him. And on today. Of all the applesaucing days! The day when I'm running unusually late to meet my boss, Freddy, at Databricks—aka the largest West Coast artificial intelligence conference. The day when Freddy and I are supposed to be first up on stage to present my research into AI neural networking. Literally the most important day of my career.

The door of Lazy Beans, the best coffee shop in all of Berkeley, was propped open to let in the cool spring breeze. Cool spring breezes are my Achilles heel, apparently. Or I'm freaking *invisible!*

Holy s'mores, nothing could be worse...

Except that when I looked up, of course, the guy who ran into me was cute. Super saucing cute. We're talking distractingly beautiful golden brown skin, deep dark eyes, and show-stoppingly sleek black hair with a hint of curl falling to his shoulders. He already had started apologizing profusely, and my smart self couldn't muster a single-word response.

"Rochelle! Oh, my god. Seriously, I am so sorry. Rochelle!" he began calling. "Make her drink again; put it on my tab." He waved at the woman behind the counter, making drinks.

The line at Lazy Beans was nearly out the door. I overheard people thrilled it was so short, but now there were grumbles of dissent that a drink was getting remade came from the line remnants. That woman seriously didn't have time to waste remaking my drink, but she threw a thumbs-up at the guy.

If my mouth caught up to my banana pudding brain, I would have laughed at his shirt hidden under layers of a zipped hoodie and olive green jacket. I think I gaped, possibly like a goldfish. Mouth flapping uselessly.

"Wanted: Dead or Alive" was printed around a cat in a box that looked like two cats, one alive and one dead. It was clever, and I am not that clever.

My phone buzzed, rattling against my car keys in my hand, and there I went, jumping like the utter scaredy cat that I am.

He'd grabbed napkins to wipe the coffee from me and then thought better of it all.

"I… oh… ok… here." He handed me the napkins.

My phone buzzed again, this time with a call. Freddy.

"I have to go!" I breathed because those were legitimately the only words that would come out of my moronic mouth, and rushed out the door. I could only hope that the day would start turning around because *this* was not a pleasant start.

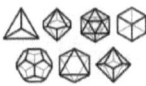

Cisco

"Cisco!" Rochelle's smile lit up the faces of those picking up their coffees. Warmer bronze skin than me and wide bouncy curls, Rochelle had an unmistakable style that I—or anyone I regularly hung out with—lacked. All I'd gleaned from her over the months of stopping at Lazy Beans since it opened was her graduation would be in a few weeks. My sixth sense (and snooping when she was on break with the other baristas) told me she was in the Business Department at the University of California.

"Almost done," she chirped and slid a cup straight to me a moment later.

"Too late. Who was the gorgeous woman I ruined the day of?" I asked as the wisps of the lingering daydream of asking the latte-drenched goddess out repeated in my head. In reality, all I could get out was an apology and repeat that twenty or more times. I'm brilliant.

Seriously, the woman was stunning. Shiny black hair tied up in a messy bun, wispy pieces falling to frame her face. And she held back shorter hairs on each side with a kawaii clip. Only up close would anyone notice there were little felt fruits on the hair clips. Her large, eyes were hidden behind adorable pale pink glasses, staring at my shirt, completely dumbfounded.

"No idea. She's not a regular." Rochelle's smile changed, and she got that sultry gleam in her eyes that made me want to try for a date with her again. "Here's her drink." And she turned the cup to make the label face me.

"Guess it doesn't matter now," I read the reprinted label. "Rina? Cool name."

Rochelle winked at me, and I have no shame in admitting it made me have thoughts.

I'd been telling my bestie, Thomas, that when I ran into gorgeous women, I would obviously ask them out. There was a plan and all, but it went COMPLETELY off the rails because of pretty eyes and stuttering conversation.

I read the rest of the label. Double shot, extra caramel, and skim milk? A conundrum. She needed extra caffeine and liked her coffee sweet, but skim milk? Did anyone drink skim because they liked it?

"Want me to start your usual? Go hop in line," Rochelle offered.

Running into a beautiful woman had to be a sign, though I really sucked at predicting whether it was a good sign or a bad sign.

As I checked my email, an incoming call from *Caleb—coworker of the century*—scrolled across the top of my phone. Scratch having a good day off the list of possibilities. I ask for five minutes to stop and get coffee to keep my sanity, and I can't even get that! Like, I already was going to be trapped in a confined space, forced to make small talk with the boss that I grew up idolizing, and the only person I have ever met that might make me snap into a homicidal rage—Caleb.

"Yes?" My jaw hurt already from clenching it shut, which was the only way to keep my words civil.

"We're running late. Dr. Wellington is most interested in the first presentation." I could hear the sneer, the insanely infuriating amount of condescension in his voice.

In. 1, 2, 3, 4, 5. Out...

"Yes, Caleb. I'm aware. Wellington also wanted coffee."

Keep your cool, Cisco. Keep it calm and...

"Why do you already have a coffee if you're in line?"

I'm pretty sure that asshole took years off my life with how far I jumped out of my skin.

"Did you seriously call me from inside the damn shop?"

Caleb... how do you describe the largest asshole you ever met? First, his face was very punchable. Pretty sure if the dude ever smiled, it'd be the first sign of the apocalypse. He constantly made everyone, but usually singled me out, feel inferior. Whether it was words that spilled out of his mouth that were nothing but insults or just the way he looked at you. Pair that with his annoying button-down shirts, pressed perfectly or perfectly swept back dusty brown hair, and thick black-rimmed glasses, and he was the catch of the century. Somehow, the man has had more girlfriends than women's numbers I have saved in my phone and... I just do not understand how.

I like to think the vibrancy and glow of my skin match my personality like his paleness and blandness matched Caleb's.

He frowned at me, and I knew the lecture coming. "You didn't answer my..."

"Bought it for a girl I accidentally ran into. Happy?" I sighed.

Caleb scanned around me very obviously not seeing anyone. "Where is this mystery woman?"

I was getting the distinct impression that Caleb did not believe me.

If I could throw in my earbuds and toss on the calming app I bought, I would have. Stupid me left the headphones in my laptop bag, and that was in the car with my boss. I sighed and tried not to be petty. "She left before the drink was made because she was late."

Caleb kept glancing between me and the label on the cup.

Oh, God! Was there any way to end this torture? Finally, I snapped, "Do. You. Want. The. Latte?"

Caleb shrugged and said simply, "I'll take it."

Chapter Two

Is this a hallucination or reality?

Rina

An AI conference is not necessarily a draw like a comic convention. I was also not entirely prepared for the Berkeley Con coming up either, but that's a whole other can of worms.

But, holy sneakers, from the back of the auditorium, the speaker on stage looked to be nothing more than a speck in each of my pictures. Maybe that's because *I'm not a photographer*. It was like Freddy knew I wouldn't be able to cut it before I arrived. All the texts I got on the way to the convention center were instructions: how to set out the pamphlets at VirTek display and where his camera was or what his good side was.

FYI: A speck has no good side.

Weeks of preparation and practice and *years* of research only to watch *my* research be presented by someone else. It wasn't even like I was scrounging for funding! Or not that I was aware of. I thought presenting at Databricks had been devised to bring VirTek up in credibility, the same as other huge labs like Infinite Labs. All I wanted was to share my findings and keep researching. I was so close to finishing the next prototypes and...

"Coffee?"

It took all my willpower not to drop the camera—which I guarantee cost more than a month's worth of my salary.

"Caleb?" Ugh, the words tasted like molding fruit in my mouth. "What do you want?"

The next stupid mistake of the day was turning, and, damn it, Caleb looked good. Well, no. Let me reiterate, he looked exactly the same as he did when we dated. Misleadingly handsome.

"Would you like this latte?" he asked.

Ok, I'm not usually this easy, and I'm not proud of accepting that coffee. But understand, the only coffee I had so far that day currently stained my shirt.

Which Caleb was now staring at. "Is that why you're not presenting *your* research?" And he pointed directly at my chest. If I didn't already know the man all too well, I would have thought he was staring at my... endowment.

"You knew I was presenting this morning?" I asked, sheepishly taking the cup and hoping he took the hint and changed the subject. I glanced at the label. Not only was it my usual latte, but it also had my name on the label. "Wait, you remember my coffee order?"

That was ridiculously sweet... What am I saying? Oh, no. I've become delusional.

"Of course, I knew you were presenting. Your research has always piqued my interest."

My research. The reminder was a slap to my face. I swear Caleb was never interested in *me* but was attracted to my research. Still, I dated worse before him... but have dated exactly no one after.

"You should go to the VirTek booth," he said with his signature hint of disinterest.

Trying to muffle a groan, I said, "I have to take pictures."

"I can take pictures for you." Caleb's eyes never left the stage or probably the slide show being presented.

"I mean, there's no point..."

"Go," he reiterated, and when he repeated himself like that, there was no arguing.

I'd found a VirTek sweater in the boxes for the booth and carried it around with me, so at least I wasn't walking around a convention center in a stained shirt. It had been hot in the auditorium, so I hadn't been wearing it. But walking the floor, I wanted to hide the stain as best I could.

The latte Caleb handed me was ice cold but honestly still delicious. I probably should stop by Lazy Beans more, but it was in the opposite direction to work and involved talking to people. Maybe if I made them an app and could order ahead.

Most of the floor was empty, with only a few stragglers meandering and picking up pamphlets from a few unmanned tables.

At the VirTek booth stood a tall man with dark brown wavy hair and a muted checkered shirt.

I really hoped Caleb didn't send me to talk to a crazy person. In the few months I had been working at VirTek alone, I had received enough of those rotten apples from coworkers. Most people who assumed I was a secretary became indignant when I corrected them.

I came up next to the guy and straightened some pamphlets. "Did you have any questions?"

"Yes, in fact." The man turned and leveled a disappointed gaze on me. "Why are you not presenting your own research?"

"Uhh...?" My brain decided, yet again, to go utterly blank.

The guy was tall, and I suck at eye contact. I tend to look to one side or above someone's head. But I had to force myself to see... holy s'mores.

"Dr. Wellington?" I gasped, finally happy I'd kept my mouth from saying anything else that would sound stupid.

"Miss Takata, you were the sole reason I made my team get up early to attend this conference. Let me guess, Mr. Carter gave you little to no notice of the change in programming."

I momentarily considered throwing my boss under the bus, but I felt lucky to have my job at VirTek in the first place. Caleb had no problem finding a job after graduation, but me? I was beat out at every turn, with hundreds of applications to companies all over the country where I was lucky if I got one phone interview before being passed over. VirTek was a startup trying to find its legs. It was a gamble, but it was also better than nothing. It floored me they were interested in AI, especially seeing as my work didn't align with their current projects.

Dr. Wellington spun around and sat on the folding table, wrinkling brochures and peering intently at me.

"Miss Rina Takata, where do you hope to go with your AI research? VirTek is far off from the arts and humanities aspect you had previously focused on."

"Excuse me?" Where was Dr. Wellington going with this? I was working on bio-substrates and increased processing power to improve efficiency and processing speed for artificial intelligence. Hardware focus, not software, and learning. Which, yes, I had primarily focused on programming and teaching aspects for AI back in my *good ole* college days.

"Those digital monster renderings were clever." The man, the myth, the legend that Dr. Wellington was... grinned at me. "Your network learned three times faster than other networks. And created artistic images with higher accuracy than the engines my people ever developed. You changed course, though, in your research."

"I..." I messed around with that stuff for fun in college. As a thought experiment and because, truthfully, who doesn't love those little characters from anime? Now, it's all the rage to see what AI can create for art or writing. "You know about that?"

"I never should have passed over you back when I hired Caleb. You two were quite the pair." Dr. Wellington's smile dimmed.

All I could answer with was a shrug and, "Caleb never cared for my programming or using AI for art."

"You'd be surprised. He admired you quite a bit, Ms. Takata. Still does. He's the reason I'm here. With this."

I hadn't noticed a rolled-up piece of paper in his back pocket until he took it out and painfully tried to unroll the paper on his lap. Dr. Wellington then said the most unexpected thing imaginable, "I was wrong to pass over you for Miss Meyers."

Now there's a name I could have gone the rest of my apple saucing life not hearing again. I like to think of myself as a kind person. Most people called me quiet and shy (they were all painfully correct). But Elise Meyers became my arch-rival first day of freshman year in college, and to this day, I couldn't tell you why.

With Elise, everything came to a head when we presented our senior theses, and she'd stolen mine right out from under me. Research and all. After many meetings behind closed doors and several votes later, neither of us was expelled. Everyone but my peers believed *I'd* stolen *her* idea. It surprised no one she got snatched up, but I didn't know it had been Infinite Labs.

Of course, instead of saying this, I said, "Is that so?"

"It was my mistake. My research into Ms. Meyers had been flawed. And I'd like to make amends for that now, Ms. Takata." The paper would never lie flat, and Dr. Wellington appeared to understand that finally and passed it to me.

While I read, Dr. Wellington continued, "If you accept my offer, you can start immediately. From what I've heard through the grapevine, I'd take that offer. VirTek has no backers to continue your research. Fred's sad attempt at diversifying has fallen pretty flat. And if you accept and need it, I will negotiate with Fred for the rights to your program and the hardware you're developing. I can see the potential Fred has overlooked thus far."

Holy s'mores. I was hallucinating. This entire day was a strange mixture of a dream and a nightmare. The salary listed was nearly double what I was making at VirTek.

"I... I..."

"You'd be working with Caleb." Dr. Wellington chuckled. "And you're the first person I feel would not..."

"Throw him through a window?" I muttered, then slapped a hand over my mouth. Oh, my banana pancakes! How did that slip out?

"Usually, people threaten far worse. And so far, no amount of money has enticed people to stay." Dr. Wellington sighed, then turned to face me. "Ms. Takata, I would like you to join us at Infinite Labs. Not because you can deal with Caleb and his own special brand of human interaction. But because you have shown yourself to be one of the most creative minds I have seen working with artificial intelligence, and honestly, you've been wasted at VirTek on hardware advancements. I believe you'll do great things no matter where you are, but

I would like a front-row seat. Think about it. HR is well-informed of the offer. All you need to do is call. We have a desk waiting for you."

Chapter Three

Breathe in, breathe out

Rina

"What do I do?" I gasped into the phone. My heart was racing. I don't even remember how the conversation with Dr. Wellington ended.

On the other end of the phone was my best (and only) friend, Audra. "First, you're going to breathe, or you're going to pass the hell out."

"This is serious!" I am pretty sure the squeal I released cracked a few panes of glass at the front of the Oakland Convention Center.

"I'm being serious! Passing out will do you no good! Remember when you signed that sketch for my dad?"

"That's not what happened." Oh, buttermilk, I couldn't do this. "There was that other woman..."

"My aunt, Rin," Audra said through gritted teeth. "My aunt."

"Audra," I felt faint. Okay, maybe—just maybe—I needed to breathe slower. Not fast and short, and... my vision was getting blurry.

Audra soothingly intoned, "In. Hold 1, 2, 3."

"Audra!"

"I don't know what you want me to say. Other than, out, 1, 2, 3."

"What should I do?" I cried.

"Infinite Labs was like *the* dream job! Go for it!" She tried to shout but also had to keep her voice down. It came out very strangled. "March into VirTek's HR office and give them your notice."

That stale, cold latte I drank was about to greet me again. "I can't do that!"

"Then you're staying at VirTek for your entire miserable career and eating up my 15-minute break. I don't know what to tell you, Rin."

I've seen people put in their notice at VirTek. It... wasn't pretty. Security would meet them less than five minutes later, tears falling down their cheeks even when they were the ones quitting.

"I put in my notice, and they'll escort me the apple fritter out of there."

Audra popped her gum and sighed, "Not your best one, sweetie."

"I'm stressed. Give me a break!"

"Rina, listen to me. VirTek has been the shittiest smart person job I have ever seen. You deserve better, and Dr. Wellington seemed cool in that presentation you dragged me to at Berkeley. Less of an ass than 'Freddy.' Like, what even is that? It's as if Fred's trying too hard to be cool."

"Audra! I can't walk in there and say, 'I... I...'—I can't even say it now!"

Audra had her breaking points with me. I heard the shuddering breath, and still, it didn't push me to actually calm down. "Rina. All you have to do is write a letter. Don't even bother going back into that God-forsaken conference or convention or whatever. Write an email, send it, and get your stuff. Did Wellington say when you can start?"

"He, uh," I stalled and crouched against a window, curling up as small as possible, I continued, "He said they had a desk waiting for me."

"Perfect. I guarantee it will take you five minutes to gather your art and other shit from VirTek and just get the hell out of there."

Audra's manager, Bill, came up behind her, and I heard him say, "It's early for Rina to be having a panic attack."

"It's an anxiety attack, Bill! There's a difference!" I screamed naturally as a few software engineers from competitors walked in with fresh coffee. I melted into a puddle of anxiety right there on the sidewalk.

"Rina. You can write an email. How did you even leave your crappy job at Equator?"

"That was *at* Berkeley. End of the academic year, they closed down. I didn't have to do anything. Plus, they knew who was graduating."

"Of course, this is your first big-girl job. Okay. Write the email before I hack into your email and write it for you." Audra's evil laugh truly rivaled those famous cartoon villains.

I'd never get a job anywhere if Audra wrote my resignation letter. I couldn't let it come to that. But how the peach cobbler was I going to write that email myself?

Cisco

"How was Databricks, Cisco?" Mandy asked the second I walked into the lunchroom. Ah, Mandy, my sweet Mandy. Not like that. I may have had the tiniest crush on her when we first met. But, alas, I am not Mandy's type. Her type is a beautiful woman, which is one of the few things I am not. The things I am are handsome, sexy, compassionate, and empathetic... I do not have a thesaurus open. Scout's honor. But it is something we can and frequently do commiserate on.

Mandy was taller than me, at least 3 inches without her heels, but she still opted to wear heels every day. Of us at Infinite, she was definitely always dressed the most professionally. Even compared to Dr. Wellington. Perfectly pressed blouses and pencil skirts and ungodly painful-looking shoes. And she had this long, perfectly curled dark blond hair she usually kept loose.

My arms were full, but I tried to toss her a sweet vacuum-sealed stainless steel travel mug with VirTek's logo. Caleb caught it and set it upright on the center island where Mandy and I ate every day.

He also drawled in his stupid, punchable way, "I do not understand the desire to have other company logos on items."

"It's free," I replied. "Would be cool to customize it." And I unloaded the rest of the items on the island. Totes and cups and squishy stress balls.

Mandy waited for Caleb to get out of earshot. "He's just jealous you didn't make him a mug."

"*You* assume he knows I customize stuff."

"You worked on them in staff meetings." Mandy slid a box of cookies over, homemade. White chocolate chip. Macadamia nuts. Drool puddled in my mouth at that first whiff. "How was the conference?"

"Good, I guess. The speaker for VirTek was changed. The dude who presented was boring as hell. It couldn't have been his research. He did *not* seem to understand the material."

"VirTek," Mandy scoffed.

Dr. Wellington has made his feelings about the company, and most of us held the same opinion with far less vehemence. VirTek was like a social experiment. The owner, Fred Carter, had already been a millionaire with a degree in buying companies or creating them and then selling them for loads of money when they became just competitive enough.

"The research was promising. I'd love to talk to that Takata person," I sat with Mandy, perusing the items I'd dropped on the island. "Whoever they are."

"Okay," Mandy's voice turned conspiratorial. "Now dish."

"Dish?" I mumbled around a cookie I'd shoved in my mouth.

"Caleb texted you when you stopped for coffee."

"Caleb texted?" The math was not adding up. Caleb wasn't social. Caleb was most assuredly a robot in human form, which needed to recharge here at Infinite at night.

"Stop it. He was pissed that you asked to stop. Even more pissed that Dr. Wellington wanted to stop, too. The schedule was going to be impacted. Then there was something about—"

No.

Mandy kept going, "—woman you ran into. And Caleb is nothing if not literal. You ran into someone. What did you do?"

"I ran into a woman." I replayed the incident. Her glasses stuck in my mind. They weren't at odds with her, per se. They were beautiful in that utterly gorgeous geeky way. And her shiny black hair, the entire ensemble (even covered in latte)... oh, she was out of my league. "Rina," I said dreamily.

"Rina...?" Mandy's smile widened, and there was absolute joy in her voice. "Dish on Rina now. Please."

"She's..." Just a woman that I would never see again, too beautiful for me to form proper sentences and who probably didn't understand the jokes I routinely wore. "She's out of my league. Ran into her and probably ruined her entire day."

"Cisco," Mandy patted my hand. "You're too hard on yourself. You know that, right?"

"It's cool." I sighed. "Rochelle said the woman isn't a regular at Lazy Beans, so I'll probably never see her again."

Chapter Four

Kitty litter

Rina

After my call with Audra, I extended my 'bathroom break,' or that is what I told Freddy when I ran from the booth after his presentation. Staying crouched against the glass and feeling woozy, I typed a resignation email. My thumb hovered over the send button, and more than a few times, I minimized the app and opened it again.

The fifth time was the charm. I hit send, almost threw up, and crawled back to my feet.

By the time I was back at VirTek's booth, Freddy was scowling at me and said, "Give me the sweater."

"What?" Mutinous tears welled in my eyes. I assumed I'd have the day. Freddy wouldn't hear until we got back to the office.

"VirTek isn't good enough for you? You thought you could come here and... what? Network?"

"I didn't..."

"No one was interested in your research, anyway. I couldn't find any buyers. Good riddance. Your stuff was garbage!" Freddy threw pamphlets at my feet. "HR will let you in just to get your stuff from your desk."

How was it *I quit*, but Freddy made me feel like I was the worst person in the world? Tears burned my cheeks as I drove. I barely remembered getting to VirTek's office and gathering my few things. A coffee mug, pictures, and my *Lazy Bean* 'You Can Do It' poster, which had been an integral part of every workday. The next thing I knew, I landed in Book Smart, the indie book store Audra worked at. Luckily, it was the end of her shift.

"I expected her here a lot earlier." I could hear the eye-roll in Bill's voice as he passed us in the cafe.

"Ignore him." Audra shooed her boss away with whispered threats. "You know what I'm wondering?"

"Don't say it." I grumbled into the table.

"What would Lazy Bean do?" Audra pulled out her own Lazy Bean travel mug from behind the counter. One of the first prototypes I'd made.

"Before or after his afternoon zoomies?" Just asking the question brought a depressed, tiny smile to my face.

"Lazy Bean had the best advice," she joked. A pencil and a little square napkin slid onto my lap. "What would Beanie say?"

"He didn't talk, Audra."

"He does now, though."

Fiiiiiine! I sat in the Book Smart's cafe sketching on napkins until Audra's shift ended. She left with me, carrying my box from VirTek to my favorite table in the cafe portion, and I read the newest Lazy Bean comic to her.

When he was actually alive, Lazy Bean had been a gray and white short hair. I kept that motif in the comic and tried my darnedest to keep his personality intact. Lazy Bean had always been an appropriate name until a mouse got into our house. Somehow, that darn cat would escape as he chased them down. Mom and I never knew how he got out of the house, but we'd get calls he was in trees or hunting on our block in San Francisco.

Audra moved into the neighboring house the year before Bean passed on. He'd often show up at her home begging for food, just like he begged my mom. Audra cried as hard as I did that day at the vet when we said goodbye.

Of all the surprises Bean brought to life, the most surprising thing about him had been he was a cat who'd actually sit with people when they cried. And Bean got plenty of practice with me.

Audra nodded along, wistful, as I read. *She* didn't cry like I would, but whenever I read a draft of Lazy Bean, I could swear her eyes turned watery.

"It'll be a hit," Audra finally said when we got to my car. Apparently, I'd been so dumb as to actually carry my entire box of stuff from VirTek into the bookstore. What kind of idiot was I?

"It's not too depressing?" I asked, looking over the jagged lines of the sketch again.

"It's exactly what Bean would do."

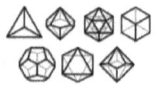

Cisco

Surprise comic drop on Lazy Bean? Can we say 'best morning ever?' Except it was some ungodly hour, and I was awake and at work, and it was entirely of my own volition.

I was in early because I couldn't sleep. After the conference, I had a brilliant idea that led me into the office in the middle of the night. Which ended after hours of simulations I didn't get to run without errors. We didn't have someone working on the AI infrastructure Wellington wanted, and somewhere in the back of my mind, I thought I could give it a go. I probably could do the coding, but I needed more time and caffeine. After encountering hurdles with the AI, my other project started plaguing my mind, too, and the two projects became one big jumble. I needed a break.

I'm stupid. I can code, build, and so on, but something about the AI structure Infinite had wasn't working, and I'll be damned if I knew what was wrong. Good thing it was only a copy on the collab site.

Wellington believed we should always have access if we got creative, and I tended to take that literally. It shocked me the first time I tried to enter the building at midnight and could, all to satisfy my curiosity about whether a new idea for a drone design would work.

Running on less than three hours of sleep was hurting me, too. The coffee was not strong enough to keep me awake, either. With my feet propped up on the conference room table, I waited for Mandy. Wellington sent out an early morning lab meeting request, and I decided I'd catch a nap in my office after that.

"Weird. Wellington doesn't do early meetings. Wonder what's going on." Mandy topped off my Lazy Bean mug (Lazy Bean curled up and sleeping on top of a laptop) with the last drops from the coffee pot in the conference room. Then, she dropped my standard handful of sugar packets next to the cup. "You gonna make it?"

"Just take notes in case I doze off."

I returned to my phone and the comic on the screen. Lazy Bean comics were usually witty, with a slap in the face of achingly relatable anxiety. Similar to comics from the 90s, but more comfort than degrading humor. It wasn't always three panels, and the surprise drop was barely one and a half. Bean's owner came home, and Bean walked over, crawled into the box next to her, and popped his head up. Then, he dropped a dead spider on her lap. In the cardboard box, Bean's owner had pictures and cups, and its labeled office. Per usual, she looks like she's been crying and pats Bean on the head.

"Thanks, Bean," she says and then screams off in a mini-panel in the corner. The title was 'Big Changes.'

Big changes? *That's it? That's all we get?* I thought.

Lazy Bean's writer has always been super elusive. People don't know much about them. It's assumed she's a woman, probably in a tech field, based on the nerdy jokes in the comic, but that could be all wrong. No one knew where they lived, what specific industry they worked in—nada. I dreamed of meeting whoever they were one day. Lazy Bean was the cat I never had, and the thoughts and feelings I've never told anyone.

Another absolutely hilarious fact was there's now a coffee shop with the same name. And yes, the name was why I went to Lazy Beans the day it opened, but I'm not ashamed to admit that I kept going because of the cute baristas.

"Aw, that's cute," Mandy coos behind me.

I sighed, gathered three packets of sugar, and ripped their tops off all at once to dump them into the black as my soul coffee.

A figure walked in. Ugh. Caleb. He wasn't a chipper any time of day, but especially in the morning, he seemed grumpier than I was.

"I'd like to give *him* the same present," I muttered, garnering a snort from Mandy.

Caleb noticed but said nothing.

The main conference room, which was not our regular meeting room, sat apart from the main lab where we generally worked. Just off from the main entrance to the building. What we lovingly referred to as the 'tourist trap' because if you were having a meeting here, you'd probably be subjected to tourists visiting the lab. Not at scarcely after 7:15 am, though.

Wellington commanded more staff than the ten people currently in the room. Whatever was going on wasn't so important that their fearless leader wanted to wait for everyone to get in. This meeting was shockingly early for Wellington, so I assumed it meant he was extremely excited about something.

"Exciting news," Dr. Wellington beamed behind his cup of coffee.

Nailed it!

"Caleb's been sold to the highest bidder?" I mumbled into my coffee.

"Close!" Wellington always heard me, no matter how quiet I tried to be. "We have a new AI Engineer starting today."

"Fifty bucks, whoever they are, they don't last a week," Mandy added, staring directly at Caleb.

We *all* blamed Caleb for the last three leaving. The last engineer didn't even make it a week.

"Now, now. It wasn't anyone's fault," Wellington stopped as a collective sigh released in the conference room. "Fair enough. Our new engineer received her master's at the same university as Dr. Williams. They worked together on their thesis at Berkeley."

"I hate when the titles get thrown around," I moaned. And I did hate it. In that room, I was the only engineer with a master's degree, not a doctorate. Caleb enjoyed rubbing it in whenever he could. "Wait. Hold up. Back up or give me more coffee."

"Not recommended, Mr. Reyes. I feel like we should relieve you before..."

"She and masters? It's a woman and *not a doctor*?" In my excitement, I nearly toppled the chair.

Suddenly, Caleb hopped out of his seat, crossed the room, opened the conference room door, and said, "We've established your ears are, indeed, functioning."

And lo and behold, in walked... coffee girl. Her hair was different, in a high ponytail and straight, and she wore another off-white flowy blouse and bright red pants. "Quit being kitty litter," she gave Caleb a low hiss.

"Everyone who is here, please welcome Miss..."

"Rina?" I blurted out.

Chapter Five

Caleb's a person (Not a robot. Weird.)

Cisco

In a conference room full of her new colleagues, I'd startled Rina without meaning to. In my defense, she was even more beautiful than I remembered. And she was here in Infinite Labs. Speaking to my mortal enemy. About an inch from his ear.

Ok, that last part was less than ideal.

"Yes, Mr. Reyes. Miss Rina Takata." Dr. Wellington presented Rina as if she were... her research! Oh. My. God! I'd realized the research... the presentation...

Dr. Wellington ignored my revelation and continued, "She comes to us from VirTek."

"And the truth comes out," Mandy said, beaming. "VirTek's presentation? You were scouting her! Not that I mind!"

Slapping Mandy's leg under the table, I hissed, "Eyes off! I met her first."

"And you have no idea how hard that is for me to give up on. She's..." Mandy stopped when Rina stared at her shoes.

In the most human gesture Caleb has ever, *ever* performed, he lightly touched her arm and whispered something in her ear. Her lips pursed, and she rolled her eyes but didn't move away.

Did my heart sink even further into a black hole when she smiled a moment later? Hell yeah, it did.

"I'd like you all to give Ms. Takata a warm welcome. Please show her around. But quietly. Mr. Reyes looks like he needs a nap." Wellington always got laughs from the doctors and engineers with quips like that.

And with that, our fearless leader excused himself. Colleagues were up and sleepily making their way to the door, giving Rina a handshake and welcome while giving Caleb a healthy dose of side-eye or outright glares.

In under a minute, or so it seemed, the conference room only contained me and my desert-like mouth, Mandy, Caleb, and Rina.

"That was... unnecessary," Rina whispered, but with the room empty, I could easily hear her.

"Wellington is ecstatic you're here." And somehow, somewhere deep within him, Caleb found the right muscles to pull a smile onto his face. "I think he wanted to have a breakfast waiting for you, but he couldn't get in early enough and didn't order yesterday. I hear he's ordering lunch, though."

Shyly, Rina dug her foot into the floor and nodded, still staring at her shoes. When she looked up and we locked eyes, my heart fluttered. I couldn't move. No, well, I could, but I worried I would dart from the room like an utter loon. Mandy shifted around me and went to introduce herself, excitedly shaking Rina's hand. The two were hitting it off while Caleb almost appeared human beside Rina.

I slowly made my way towards the door, desperately clutching my Lazy Bean mug in a death grip. Either I'd talk to Rina and be suave, or I'd be an idiot. It was a coin flip at this point.

Rina tilted her head and gave me a shy smile. "Hi," she said and waved. And took a tentative step back. "I'm wearing a light color again."

"Yes, we have all heard of Cisco's brilliant accident," Mandy said and slid into uninhibited laughter effortlessly.

"Cisco?" Rina asked.

"R-R-Reyes," I stuttered.

Rina

Caleb gave me a tour around Infinite Labs, which was extensive compared to the cramped office and tiny lab spaces VirTek owned. People streamed in and actively avoided Caleb. Literally not a surprise. In fact, I might have giggled the second time it happened and said, "Some things never change, huh?"

Instead of giving me heck, Caleb grinned, too. "I've gotten used to it."

I'm not used to Caleb smiling. And I don't think anyone around me was used to it either.

He ended the tour at my new office.

Rina Takata was right next to the door on a small placard.

"How...?"

"Dr. Wellington was fairly sure you'd accept. I'm glad you did."

Well, sometimes surprises come from the most surprising places. I laughed. "You're never happy about anything."

"Dr. Wellington mentioned you said as much. I *always* loved being with you."

Caleb and I dated for nearly eighteen months, and never once in that time did Caleb tell me he loved me. He didn't tell me he loved anything. The singular word coming out of his mouth sent a huge flush to my cheeks. Oh my buttermilk pancakes, I was burning up and over what? My apple saucing ex-boyfriend?

"Get settled. Dr. Wellington wants to speak to us about the project's existing AI infrastructure and staffing. We'll be reallocating resources," Caleb said, still with his strange smile.

"For... me?"

Finally, his facade cracked. "Yes, Rina," he said impatiently.

Holy muffins.

Cisco

"Why are you whining so loudly?" Mandy asked from the door of my office. "I thought you'd trapped a dying animal in here while napping somewhere else."

"Did you see them?" I pushed off and let my desk chair take me in a lazy circle.

"Who?"

"Caleb and Rina." I couldn't get her name out without that dreamy quality.

"Yeah, ok. I'll admit that was weird. Caleb's acting strange."

"Like a person?" Those words regarding Caleb were so bitter in my mouth.

"Yes! One with actual feelings and everything. I don't like it."

"Oh, for the love of apple sauce, Caleb." Dost my ears deceive me? That sounded like Rina. "I need to review all the tax forms and agreements and stuff. I'm not looking at the collab right now."

"Rina, you are fully capable of running it in the background," Rina cut off Caleb with a stamp on the tiled floor and a muffled scream.

I ran to the door to catch her slamming an office door in Caleb's face.

"Hope is renewed," I breathed.

"Lord, it's going to be a rollercoaster with you. I should have shot my shot," Mandy said with a sigh.

Chapter Six

Bean mug purloiner

Cisco

Pings from my phone woke me, and the bright screen assaulted my eyes.

> Mandy: What happened?

> Mandy: Talk to me!

> Mandy: I will come down there and flick your ear until you answer me. So just do us all a favor and **answer me!**

It's not like my status was, "Going to rot and die in the bio lab." This had been, legit, the worst day. Capped off with my Lazy Bean mug mysteriously vanishing.

Mandy: Whatever it is, it can't be that bad.

Cisco: It's that bad.

Mandy: Based on the dirt I have, **IT CAN'T BE!**

Yes, it could be that bad. I spent the last day working myself up to talk to Rina, and she snapped as soon as I said hi. She probably didn't intend to snap at me. I had barely interacted with her over the two days she'd been at Infinite Labs since she was engrossed in all those papers HR gives you, getting her office set up, etc. But there was *no way* I could show my face in front of Rina again.

Cisco: What dirt?

The question was so obviously a mistake the moment I typed it.

Mandy: Dirt like… Rina and Caleb dated.

Oh God, that was so much worse.

Mandy: Talk to me.

Ignoring Mandy would earn me the icy Mom glare she'd already perfected without having kids yet and cornering me, which I probably deserved. Still, I needed a break and to be out of my office. I scouted around each corner as I made my way to the break room. Mostly, I was trying to avoid Rina. Tomorrow would be another day and another attempt, assuming she didn't totally brush me off like she had today.

Oh my god, what if she was still pissed about the coffee? What if I screwed up any chance just by running into her?

I forced myself to stop. The coffee incident was an honest mistake. *Rina dated Caleb?*

Really? Rina, goddess of the cute geeky girls, dated Caleb "no one will ever be better than me" Williams?

That was what she found attractive? That stuck up, lanky...

I was screwed. Completely, totally, sincerely screwed. What would Rina ever see in me? I wasn't built with long, lean muscles. I'd never, ever have a six-pack. Hell, there was no way I'd have a two-pack. Sure, I had muscles, but everything lacked definition since I'd rather read comics and play a video game than pick up a free weight.

Also, I usually (like now) garnered lots of strange stares from friends and strangers alike. At the moment, it was for scouting around corners like I was the hero in a spy movie. But sometimes you have to do what you have to do. Luckily, I never ran into Caleb or Rina.

And thankfully, not Mandy, either.

When I got to the break room, I brewed a new pot of coffee and paced around the island as I waited until a cup caught my eye. The unmistakable swish of a cat's tail coming from around the other side of the cup. Contorting to read the side of the mug, instead of turning it around like a normal person, I read, *It's a purr-fect day for a nap.* And Lazy Bean laid across an entire desk full of notes and a keyboard and mouse.

Hold the freaking phone. Who the hell was also a fan of Lazy Bean, and *how did they have a mug I didn't have?*

What if they took my mug? Oh... OH, HO HO! This meant war.

Rina

The first couple of days at Infinite were spent getting caught up on how things are done in this office, schedules, paperwork, and learning their systems and conventions (the boring kind, not comic ones). Also, those days were filled with strange ups and downs with Caleb. Maybe it was because we weren't dating anymore that made it easier to deal with his crud. Slamming the door on him didn't deter him like I always feared.

He'd come back an hour later with a sheepish grin and a peace offering of coffee, and we'd keep working.

Everyone else in the lab, barring Dr. Wellington, stepped on eggshells around Caleb. Which I totally understood. In part, it was his position—or it was his demeanor. Most engineers reported to him. Technically, I reported to him too. But for the first time in my life, that didn't matter when I couldn't stand his garbage attitude any longer and snapped.

It all figured I would screw up when I let my emotions get the better of me.

To be completely fair, I realized I snapped. It wasn't me, or like me. But Caleb kept interrupting me while I was trying to get a basic grasp on this new... new... EVERYTHING and I was positive that Wellington realized the mistake he'd made hiring me because I was having trouble getting anything to work and getting my paperwork in order and... *I sucked!*

A mug of steaming coffee appeared next to my arm. The heat radiated into my muscles and even my bones. I'd been sitting, burying my face in my hands, trying to calm down and not break into utter hysterics on my second day.

When I pulled my hands away from my face, Caleb stared down at me, his face neutral.

"What's this?" I asked.

"Coffee."

"I know," I stopped myself before I snapped again. It was bad enough that I 'apple sauced' in front of Cisco, and he went scurrying away. "Where'd you get this mug?"

"It's your mug," Caleb answered, already losing patience again.

"What do you mean?" I was too tired for games.

"You created Lazy Bean," Caleb stated as if I'd forgotten.

"I know that. Where did you get *this* mug?" *And how did he know I created Lazy Bean?*

"Isn't it yours?" He frowned at the mug. "It was in the break room."

I spun the mug around. It *was* a legit Lazy Bean mug. Bean's butt staring the user in the face with the text, "Wake me when I'm needed." The cup was a first run. One of the first merch I ever made for Bean.

"This is from my manufacturer. Like an actual run of Bean merch." Caleb didn't seem to understand what I was saying. "I only use my homemade prototypes since I don't sell those."

Generally, I gave the samples away from the manufacturer or raffled them off and used my homemade prototypes since they were extra special. Lately, I'd been using one I had scrapped the idea on. I thought it was funny, but Audra wasn't so sure. Bean always laid across my desk and all my homework when I was in school. It was so appropriate. And if he were with us today, it would have been the same with my thesis and even work now. Audra had a point that this new prototype was too close to some of the other designs I had in my store.

Caleb kept watching me as if I were speaking Latin. Except if I *were* speaking Latin, he'd understand.

"Who else has one?" I asked.

He didn't do shrugs. Caleb glanced down at the cup with his eyebrows lifted.

I left Caleb sitting in my office amongst my piles of papers and went to the break room where I'd left my mug.

Above the stainless steel sink, someone had taped a note, "This means war. I confiscated your Bean mug until the purloiner of mugs returns *my* Bean!"

Chapter Seven

Which came first? The comic or the coffee shop?

Rina

"Where. Is. My. Mug?" I was out of breath when I got back to my new office.

Still sitting in my guest chair, Caleb barely spared me a glance. He didn't even acknowledge my existence.

"Caleb!"

He turned my mug and holy... shitake; it took everything not to punch him in the nose.

"Where?" I threw the note at his face. Not forcefully or anything. I've never been the athletic type. But at least I hit him in the face.

"Office... 207, if I had to hypothesize based on the handwriting..."

Caleb most likely kept talking, but I was already out the door and turning in circles, trying to figure out where 207 was. I started in one direction and realized the numbers were going the wrong way. I was in office 221 (yes, I considered making a sign honoring Sherlock Holmes) and had to turn back around when I saw office 226.

Blind to the signs, except for numbers, I threw open the door and demanded, "Where's my mug?" I probably make it sound so much more forceful than it was.

"Well, well, well," the person in the chair, mimicking every drama-queen villain ever, spun slowly until he faced me and then dropped my mug. "Rina!" Cisco exclaimed and scrambled to pick up the cup, thankfully undamaged, from the floor.

No. Nope. Not happening. Oh, my hands shook, and I lost my train of thought. Why did I come all the way down here? What... oh, my mug. Oh, for muffin's sake! Why did *he* have to take my mug? Wait...

"This is yours?" he squeaked.

For the love of blueberry muffins, my brain didn't know what else to focus on except the note that I left balled up in my office. "I thought you said this meant war?"

If I could, I would have hidden until the end of time. We're talking quit my brand new shiny job, move to—I don't know—another planet.

After a few silent mouth flaps, Cisco asked, "You like Lazy Bean?"

I nodded dumbly, and he kept going, eyes narrowing on me. "Where did you get this? It's never been released. I know. I looked."

Suddenly, I felt stupid for keeping a listing of all the back merch on the Bean website.

"I... I... I..." Brilliant brain! I was back to stuttering in front of the cutest guy ever that I now *worked* with!

"Are you really that huge of a Bean fan?" Cisco hopped to his feet. "Have you seen some of the Lazy Bean fanart on... well... are you even on..."

"Yes," I said, though it sounded like a question. The only places I lurked on the web were my website and the more art-centered blogging sites. Putting my mind to Bean and the incredible fanart I received got me over the hump of trying to talk to a cute guy. "The fanart of Bean is awesome. There are a few artists I follow."

"Finally!" He fell back, spinning in his chair. "No one here gets Bean! They think it's ridiculous that I read him."

"You mean Caleb thinks..."

"Yes! Caleb is the worst. I don't know how you're going to put up with him. Oh, what's your favorite comic?"

"Uh, favorite?" Can you have a favorite of your creations? I guess that's possible, but I can't answer that on command. I've never thought about it. *Son of a bean, are these the questions I was going to get at the con?* "I mean... I..."

"You don't have to answer," Cisco said, and froze up.

Bisquits, what did I say? Shoot!

It would have been rude to take my mug from him and walk away. Ugh! This! I was the absolute worst at dealing with people. Plucking the first comic that came to mind, I said, "I love the ones where he lays across his owner's keyboard. Like she can't do anything and... he forces her to do... something else...?"

Letting out a breath he'd been holding, Cisco continued, unfortunately, with less enthusiasm. "He's always making her do the things she doesn't want to do."

Literally, and then cleaning up a disgusting hairball five minutes later. Those things only made it into the comic a few times, but I couldn't hold back a little laugh at the thought. If Bean were here now, he'd hock one up now on Cisco's shoes.

There was this laugh that Cisco had. It brightened his entire face and was almost childlike in how ecstatic he became. I couldn't help but smile, too. Maybe, since he laughed, I hadn't totally screwed up.

"So… trivia." Cisco swallowed a lump but kept going. "Which came first: the comic or the coffee shop?"

Oh, no. Blushing was next. And I wasn't the cute blusher. When I blushed, it looked like a patchy sunburn gone wrong. I stared at my shoes when I answered, "The comic. The coffee shop owners loved the comic so much they named their shop after it, and…" Goodness, this was embarrassing. "A drink."

"Have you had a Bean?"

I may or may not have changed my usual order after having a Bean. It was great… I just… couldn't handle having a drink named after my little Bean. And since Lazy Bean was out of my way for VirTek, I didn't feel guilty for not stopping to get a drink named after my comic.

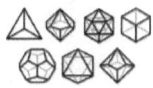

"It got so awkward." In fact, when I got back to my office, I kicked Caleb out and said I had a breakthrough, then hid in there crying until the end of the day. Crying about paperwork, but also… Cisco.

"I bet it did," Audra giggled. "You're always awkward."

I buried my face into a throw pillow and screamed.

"What was that?" Audra laughed even harder.

"I can't show my face at work again. Maybe Dr. Wellington will let me work remotely," I sobbed, "in Greenland."

"How many charms did you make for the con?" Audra threw another pillow at me. "And you would probably rather work in Iceland."

Muffled by the pillow, I answered, "150."

"Books?" She continued through the checklist, barely acknowledging my utter breakdown.

Still muffled by the pillow, "Loaded in the trunk already."

"Ah, your brother stopped by?"

Audra wasn't taking this seriously! "What am I going to do?" I whined.

"Apparently, you are planning to give up on the best job you could ever hope to have because you can't talk to a cute boy." Audra seemed to consider something, humming to herself.

"He's a man."

"Correction, cute man." I could hear Audra's absolute delight at this whole ordeal. "I know. You could quit and come work at the bookstore where you have to talk to people all day. Maybe it will work like therapy..."

"Why is it the best job?" I'd finally decided to unbury my face. "I mean... I like it."

"Please! You can deal with Caleb and his shi— his pancakes, so no, they won't ever get rid of you. Perfect job." Audra leaned over closer, her voice turning sultry. "I need to meet this cute man. See what all the hype is about and what's got you flustered. And then thank him."

I had never whipped a pillow so wildly across the living room of my tiny apartment, and never had I been so reckless. The metal stand on which my crafting printer and cutter sat wobbled, and my heart almost stopped entirely.

"Oh, I really need to meet this guy. He's under your skin, girl. And that... that is saying something. Because you *never* get smitten."

"I am not smitten!" I screeched.

Audra snorted, "You are so smitten!"

I re-buried my face in the pillow and tried to steady my breathing. My cheeks were officially on fire again.

"Rina? Rina!" Audra appeared before me, bent, and pulled the pillow out of my grasp. "Smitten is good. It's been a long time since you and Caleb broke up. Dating someone would be good for you."

"Who said anything about... about... dating?" No! I was not going to date *anyone*! Let alone someone I worked with. That... that would be...

"Your cheeks. Your stuttering and screaming into a pillow and... well, pretty much everything about how you look right now." With that, she moved on to another box and asked, "How many mugs?"

I threw myself down again and stared at my cruddy apartment's ancient, stained ceiling. "Limited edition. 50 of each con design." Nothing was stopping the fire. How in the world was I going to work with someone who did *this* to me?

Audra carried a box to the dolly at the front door, and hoping she wasn't in earshot, I mumbled, "Can't date someone you can't talk to."

Chapter Eight

Comic can't

Rina

"Oh, perfect timing! Rin! Sign!" Audra tossed a Bean book on top of my salad box and started counting change.

"What's going on?" I asked in a hushed, yet I thought clearly aggravated tone.

"Audra brought you a gift. I 1000% support it," Haru's devilish grin dampened by his long, scruffy curly black hair. If brothers were the worst, Haru lorded over all other brothers.

Hastily, I scratched out a signature, hoping no one could actually read my name. I drew a quick Bean face, then went about flipping over the signs on the table until I found it.

Meet the creator! Be sure to ask for an autograph!

"I hate you." I pinched the corner of the sign and yanked it from the plastic sign holder I'd been using to list prices.

In a most cheery way, Audra sang, "You love me for taking time out of my *busy* schedule to be here and help you out."

"You signed me up for the convention," I shot back at Audra amidst Haru's fit of giggles that turned into full-on gasping chortles.

I looked at Audra, then my brother, then back. Audra was nearly bursting, too. "Haru signed you up," she said between her own giggles.

Taking the sign, I tore it into strips right in Audra's face. A few people, some dressed in pancake-flipping fantastic cosplays and browsing my books and charms, joined in on the laughing.

"Rina, you didn't even work the table yesterday." Haru's comment was punctuated by a spray from a cherry tomato he crushed between his teeth from my salad in his mouth.

"And you barely sold anything," I hissed back at Haru.

Brothers were the literal worst. Haru's jaw dropped and he pointed at the boxes behind the table. "We sold almost half..."

A loud whooshing in my ears drowned everything around me out. I clamped my hand on the marker I'd used to sign that last book and felt my chest become heavier.

No. Not now! Nope!

It was one thing to go to a con and be around a lot of strangers who loved my comic (and tried to talk to me at length), but it was quite another when you saw someone you knew. Or I thought I did.

This was not happening. Other than Caleb, whom I did not care what he thought about my Lazy Bean comic, no one at Infinite knew I had the comic. I'd even successfully kept it a secret when I was at VirTek. I'd planned to keep it hidden until the day I died, if at all possible.

But.. Long black hair, not much taller than me, plaid shirt... ridiculously sweet, compassionate brown eyes.

I blinked, and Cisco was gone.

Waving her hand in front of my face, Audra said, "She's gone."

"I-I-I," I kept stuttering and dropped the marker. A girl in a cute blue and white uniform and asymmetrical brown bobbed wig held The Bean, Volume 2 (where Bean laid in place of the famous monument in Chicago).

"She's waiting for you," Haru said, shaking my shoulder.

But the movement jarred me, and I saw him again through the crowd of Artist Alley.

"Gotta p—use the bathroom!" I couldn't even fake a smile. I ducked out from behind the tables and pushed through the crowd, my heart hammering. I felt faint and barely made my way into the women's bathroom.

The stalls were filled. But I found a baby changing station at the back unoccupied and curled into the corner just as Audra came barreling through, ignoring protests of people waiting in line.

"Rina? Rina! What happened?" Her phone trilled at max volume, but she cut the tone off.

Her calls to me stopped. I thought maybe I was home free to have a panic attack in peace, but when I peered through my hands, Audra had bent down to meet me at my eye level.

"What's going on?" she asked me, her hands gently circling my wrists.

"He's here." Two words were all I could manage through shuddering breaths.

"Who's here?" But Audra ran out as fast as she'd come in when she realized who I meant. Best friend, my tushy.

Cisco

"Holy shit, dude. Your comic has a table here!" Thomas, the best man I know and current dungeon master for our D&D game, rapped on my shoulder. We were currently wandering Artist Alley, and he pointed at the end table for the row we were entering.

Neither of us had the chops to make a cosplay (we tried, and my brother made fun of us the *whole* time). To be fair, Thomas could pull off any cosplay. The dude was the cool, chic kind of geek. Stylish, shaggy blond hair combed forward, the right amount of stubble, clear plastic frames, and tall. Girls *apparently* were attracted to men taller than them. Or that had been my experience thus far.

A vinyl sign draped over the table showed Bean's butt lifted into the air, ready to pounce on a computer mouse. I could imagine what Bean's cute, cartoony owner may do, but they weren't pictured on the sign.

"I'll just..."

Thomas flashed a grin at some unsuspecting cosplayer, who fawned. "You'll be spending all your cash at the Bean table?"

"I will be... spending... a lot of money..." I wiped some drool from my chin.

"Go." Thomas shooed me away. "Maybe the creator's there, and you can..."

The guy at the table slipped a new sign into a plastic stand.

Meet the creator.

Though he also added a sticky note: *Soon.*

"Get an autograph?" I finished for Thomas, my heart racing a million miles a minute.

Swerving and sliding around the crowd in Artist Alley, I made it unscathed to the table and piled Bean merch in my hands. Charms, a couple of stickers, the two books, and a bookmark.

"When's the creator coming?" I asked, trying not to sound overly eager.

I guarantee I failed miserably.

"I think I jinxed it." The guy totaled the merchandise (less than I assumed I'd spend, but there was less Bean merch than at most other vendors). "But try coming back. She's been around but hates the attention."

The only appropriate and manly response I had ready was, "Aw." I insist that it was a manly 'aw' and no one can take that away from me.

"You know you got two of the same cell charms, right?" The guy behind the table didn't help a thing. He was distractingly and unfairly handsome, like a J-pop or K-pop star with that bowl-cut wavy hair and slender frame.

"Yeah. One's for," I turned and saw Thomas chatting with a female artist specializing in anime characters. A standing tower showcased tons of 8x10 art prints with colorful ombre backgrounds and a single character on each. I recognized more than half, and all the characters had a more cartoony appearance than the anime artist's design. "One's for my coworker. She really likes Bean, too."

Unfairly handsome potential K-pop star winked at me. "Go get 'em, tiger."

Rina

Haru eventually convinced the many women in line he was just coming to get his deranged sister from the bathroom post-panic attack. And when that didn't work, flirting did. He stooped to ruffle my hair, so I responded with a slap to his legs.

"It's been a half-hour." Haru then pinched my ear. "Whoever was coming that you didn't want to see you here is long gone."

At this point, I was not sure there was a reason to leave this bathroom corner other than food, but I could probably pay someone to deliver that to me from the food court.

"People want to meet the cool woman who created Lazy Bean." Apple streudal! Haru went from annoying brother to kind of sweet.

Still, I wasn't giving in. I pointed to the sky.

"God, not God!" Haru took my wrists and yanked me up to my feet. "Come on."

At the table, Audra's overly wide smile struck a nerve. "I have more news."

"I can't handle more news."

Chapter Nine

Cute guy from work

Rina

More news was not good news, no matter what spin Audra tried to put on it. And yes, I dwelled. That's what I do best, after all.

Lazy Beans Book Signing at Book Smart

"Why?" I asked for the umpteenth time.

"You spent more of the con hiding than meeting fans."

"I said you'd get more money. And then you can move out of that crap-hole apartment," Haru added because, of course, my brother was Audra's co-conspirator. I bet he even made the call to Audra's manager. Sweet talked him and everything.

I tried not to choke Haru. "This is the first day I've been at the con!"

"And you spent a lot of it in the bathroom already," he answered while also waving at a few girls who giggled on their way past the table.

The rest of the weekend flew by and I crashed hard Sunday night.

On top of the 'news', the never-ending parade of fans, and bloat-inducing con food, returning to work—no, just rolling out of bed Monday morning—was nay impossible. No one told me that working or attending a comic convention would be so exhausting. Audra was right; I mostly sat at the table or cowered in a bathroom for two days. That shouldn't have constituted such exhaustion.

Dr. Wellington never set strict times for us to be in the lab, but I preferred to get in early and get home early. After the convention, I was lucky to haul myself in at the ripe old time of 8:30 a.m., in as put-together of a state as I could manage. Between shuffling my coffee, laptop, and notes, I scrawled on napkins at the con for the AI. I stopped dead when I set down my coffee, and it tipped.

Where I always set my coffee mug sat a Bean charm. One of the charms I sold over the weekend was a con exclusive. And underneath the charm, a sticky note read: *Thought you'd like this. -Cisco*

As soon as I met Audra at Book Smart on Tuesday evening, she caught the charm dangling on my phone. Probably because she'd been selling them all weekend.

"You advertising your own brand? Finally?" She carried a box of new books down the aisle to unload.

"No," I squeaked and hid the keys in my fists, debating which would be harder: lying to Audra or taking the charm off.

The sing-song voice returned. "Is it from work-guy that you think is *cuuuuuuuuute*?"

"I hate you," I said, rushing around the manga section, grabbing the newest releases, and trying to avoid Audra's rampant giggles. Of course, that meant I stopped looking where I was going and rammed book pile first into someone so hard we both fell on our... derrieres.

"How is it you're such a geek? You can't even walk around a book-shelf without screwing up?"

My heart hammered. Like, about to explode from my chest, reminiscent of high school torture, hammered.

"I am so, *so* sorry," a guy said. Was that voice overly familiar?

"Cisco?" I looked up, and... okay... chest was now on fire, heart hammering, I might go into cardiac arrest.

"Here." He hastily piled the books on bent knees and whistled at the titles. "Oh! Is this..." And that was where he faltered.

"Come on, *manito*. We're not here for your comics."

The other guy had an air about him. Suave, perfectly styled, and waved black hair, a crisp Oxford shirt. He could practically be a runway model. And Cisco withered before him, absently running his hands through his long hair over and over.

Something came over me. In a word, it was stupidity. "Cisco? You didn't mention you were bringing your..."

"Brother?" he finished. "I've... told you so much about Santiago." Cisco held half my pile of books. I kept the other half. He leaned closer to my ear, and I swear I burped bile. "What are you doing?"

"Thought we were getting *mami's* birthday gift. Let's move. I don't want someone to catch me with *you*." Santiago was slower on the uptake than Cisco. An eerie shiver passed through me when he gave me a look up and down. "Hello," Santiago drawled in what I assumed was meant to be a sexy tone. He even swept up my free hand and brushed his lips against my knuckles like it was some romance movie. "Estás preciosa!"

"You're not fooling..." Cisco tried to whisper but I cut him off when I grabbed Cisco's arm, lacing mine through and gripping so hard my muscles ached.

And somewhere, something deep inside of me snapped. Though my knuckles turned white clutching my manga stack, I mustered enough braincells to say, "You didn't tell your family yet, right?"

Cisco's brother growled, "*Manito?*" Santiago was obviously a guy that had never once been rebuffed.

Slowly, Cisco began to play along. "I... did... not."

I lost all sense. I have no idea what came over me. But I clenched my stomach, prayed I'd be okay for a few minutes, and pecked Cisco on the cheek.

Cisco

Santiago has never — I mean *never* — been so confused in his entire life. I mean... *I* was confused when Rina kissed my cheek, but Santiago had never had his charms not work on a woman before.

When he found his voice again, Santiago practically choked on his next words, "You have a girlfriend? *You?*"

"I... do?" The air in my mouth grew extra weight and I choked on it. "I do!"

I did not expect Rina's iron grip on my arm, which made it throb. Trying to release myself from her and put my arm around her waist was impossible with her iron grip.

"Well. Isn't that... fantastic. You, *manito*, should bring—"

"Rina," Cisco supplied helpfully.

"—*Rina*, to mamí's birthday party."

Surprisingly, she beamed at him. "I'd love to."

"Fantastic. *You* get *mamí's* present," Santiago wore a tense smirk and stormed out of the bookstore.

"Wow. Wooooow! Rina? That was..."

Her books fell to the floor again as she darted toward the bathroom.

"Rina?" a woman in a distressed shirt that read "Comic!" in an action bubble and bright red glasses called from the corner of non-fiction. Her thick dark brown hair was pulled into a high ponytail, and her light tan skin wasn't much different from his own. "Oh, no." And she went chasing after Rina.

I followed, skidding to a stop at the door to the women's bathroom, and heard retching. "Whoa."

"It's okay, Rin." The girl's voice echoed in the bathroom. She knocked softly on the door. "I'm here."

Good, because I was about ready to vomit just hearing her retch. It was a flaw for me. That sound incited a reaction, and... it wasn't pretty after.

"Is Rina okay?" I asked the other girl when she came out of the bathroom.

"She'll be fine. Eventually." She smelled her hand and grimaced. "Uh, do you know what happened?"

"What do you mean?" I tried to look behind her into the bathroom but heard another loud retch.

"Well, if she's puking, she did something that like super stressed her out. And she's mumbling on repeat about being dumb so...?"

Oh. OOOOOH. Oh, my God. I never should have played along. "Does pretending to be my girlfriend count as stressful?"

The woman pinched her lips together and looked me up and down. "Huh." Her hip popped out and a devious smile spread across her lips. "I'm buying you coffee."

"What?" My voice cracked... again. *Every time Reyes! What is it with you when girls talk to you?*

This woman gave me an appraising look. "You're the 'cuuuuuuute guy from work.' And this is going to be good when Rin comes back out. I need to get my manager, too."

The books slipped out of my hands, and I struggled to pile them back in my arms before they landed on the ground. "Wait, why?"

"He's never going to believe he gets to meet you. And he's going to have a field day with this."

"What about Rina?"

"Other people don't help when she's having a panic attack or anxiety attack. She just gets more embarrassed. Better to be prepared with soda water to calm her stomach."

The bookstore clerk moved away from the bathroom and beckoned me to follow. But my mind caught up, and I dropped the books in a pile on the ground. "Did you say, 'cute guy from work'?"

Chapter Ten

Pulling out the big guns

Rina

Audra kicked the bathroom door open, and the way it boomed on the wall nearly set off a whole new panic attack in me.

"Good, you're feeling better. Short, long dark hair, and actually very cute, is sitting in the cafe."

"Blueberry muffins..." I muttered.

"And my girl is back," Audra cackled.

"... why is Cisco still here?" No amount of breathing or vomiting had helped, but I knew screeching wouldn't either. Yet here I was, in hysterics, screeching and then slapping my hands over my mouth.

I blinked. Audra grinned. And kept grinning. "I bought him coffee."

"Why?" New tears and sobs were imminent.

"Because I had questions, and you were in here panicking." Audra's casual grin was laced with calm. "Answers were needed. Like, if he was at the con."

I ran out of the bathroom, rounded past the magazines, and saw Cisco making his way through the synopsis of each manga in my pile. Sitting at *my favorite* table in the cafe.

Audra sauntered past the cafe, swinging her keycard. "Oh, and you better buy those. You banged them up good. Hi, Cisco, my man."

Oh, that's good. Audra had it in for me! But she barely went past the cafe's entrance and came back only a few moments later with a life-size cardboard standee of... me?

"You like it?" My best friend must be an evil villain. Maybe Lazy Beans could have an archnemesis in his life and I could base everything about the archnemesis on Audra!

"Uh... Rina?" Cisco dropped the newest issue of a superhero manga on the table. "What... are you... doing on..."

Audra literally stopped right in front of Cisco, showing off the standee like a game show hostess.

Meet Lazy Bean's creator! Signing on Saturday!

"You... you... you're..." Cisco stammered.

I was ready to run back to the bathroom until Audra grabbed my arm.

"Cisco, you, my friend, missed out on *meeting* Rina at the con this weekend. Discuss." Audra slapped my back, making me stumble forward. "Good luck. You need to do this. And hopefully, your stomach is empty, so no more vomit."

If I wasn't absolutely petrified, I would maim Audra with the soda water she left out for me on the table. Even if she was the best for having said soda water ready.

Audra moved the standee to the front window despite my moans of protest. "You'll be fine. Invite 'cute work boy' to sit with you on Saturday."

"You created Bean?" Cisco's voice began achieving new octaves.

There was no way I could look at him. I'd screwed up so, so bad! He was going to hate me for not telling him before, and I had every single chance. Biscuits. Streudal. Pie. Pancakes! GAH! I couldn't look anywhere near Cisco.

A rhythmic tapping pulled my attention to his hands on the table. "Guess that makes sense with the mug." No! Now disappointment wormed its way from Cisco into me as he continued, "And it was silly to give you the charm."

On another pass, presumably back to doing actual work, Audra said, "Check her key chain, cute work boy!"

Clamping down on my lips, praying Audra had been right and no vomit could possibly be left in my stomach, I held my hand up. The keys dangled from my finger.

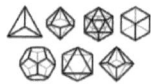

Cisco

There was a dichotomy to Rina that I didn't expect. I guess I always thought she was so confident. Cool and aloof when I crashed into her at the coffee shop, she was very assured of herself when she started at Infinite Labs. Even the way she handled Caleb all the time didn't scream anxiety.

And here I was, an anxious mess whenever I planned, thought about, or actually talked to her.

Sure enough, Audra was right. I lifted my eyes to almost meet Rina's and saw the charm on her key chain.

Since we were out of the danger zone, considering Santiago had left the bookstore, I hopped off the three steps up to the cafe and handed her the bottle of grape soda water.

"I've been stressing about talking to you. Like every day." I admitted sheepishly.

Still looking a little green, Rina attempted to smile. "That's crazy. I'm not anything special."

What a bold lie that was. "If you weren't special, do you think Dr. Wellington would have gone out of his way to recruit you?" Rina avoided eye contact, staring instead at the books on display near the cafe or the counter behind my head, all while blushing. "I mean, anyone who can deal with Caleb for more than two minutes has a superpower. So..."

Rina turned to face me, and sure, there were blotchy patches on her face, and her makeup was a bit washed off. It didn't matter. Rina didn't need that to look beautiful.

"Want to sit with me?" She pointed at the table Audra had steered me towards earlier.

"She does!" Audra screamed from some unknown part of the store.

"Shut up, Audra!" Rina said louder than I'd heard her all evening.

"OOOOOH!" Still out of sight, Audra yelled back, "She pulled out the big guns!"

"That's right," I pressed my lips together to stop from laughing. "I've never heard you swear. Not even when Caleb is being... Caleb. Which is incredible because everyone swears at Caleb."

"I... don't." Her eyes were glassy. "Swear, that is. And you don't have to. Sit with me. Or the birthday party and... I'm sorry about earlier. I hope I didn't mess things up. I just..."

Oh, no. "Had plenty of people call you a nerd?" Rina's head jerked up at me, and a quiver shook her lip. "Give you shit for reading comics and being an adult? Stole every girl you ever liked?"

Fresh tears made her eyes glassy. "Yes, exactly! Except the last one...?"

Rina

Audra kept passing by the cafe. I still felt like vomiting, but sitting with Cisco made it... less terrible.

I sketched on napkins when I had trouble meeting his eye. "Bean was my cat. Well, for most of my life."

"So, are the comics true?" He'd laid his chin on his hands and watched me draw.

"Some. People always made fun of me, including Haru, for talking to Bean. But Bean didn't make fun of me for crying or having a panic attack or anxiety attack. He'd always come and sit on my lap until I calmed down."

Cisco finished his coffee a while ago. I'd taken the cardboard sleeve and sketched Bean in different stages of catching a butterfly.

"Yeah, well, I wish I'd had a pet like Bean. Santiago gives me shit for reading comics, clearly. There is no respite, even at work with assholes like Caleb." He slapped a hand over his mouth. "Sorry. I..."

"I don't mind." I smiled. My chest finally loosened up and I'd finished the soda water. "Saying things like 'blueberry pancakes' gets me heck too."

"She's obsessed with baked goods!" Audra screamed... again!

Cisco fiddled with the pile of manga, straightening them, moving stuff around on the table, and taking some deep breaths. "Would you... want to come to my mom's birthday party?"

Okay, I tried not to let my breathing turn to hyperventilation. I'm not sure how well that worked.

"You don't have to," he said quickly. "I can tell my family you're busy and..."

"I started the problem by telling your brother we were dating." Adding a few accent lines, I showed Cisco a sketch of Bean and a birthday cake. One he'd jumped into on my 17th birthday.

Because my brain is working against me.

"You don't have to go to the party." Cisco rubbed the edge of the coffee sleeve with his finger. "I just thought it would be nice... and I could maybe take you out to a movie or a park or..."

"She sits in her apartment and does nothing but craft and write Bean comics. TAKE THE WOMAN OUT!" Clearly, there was nowhere in the store Audra couldn't hear them. "And we're closing in five minutes. Get the hell out after paying for your haul, girl!"

"Like... a date?" I twisted the felt-tip marker I carried around in my pocket that I'd been sketching with.

Cisco smiled, and he absolutely had the same smile as his brother, only there was still that sweet, ecstatic quality. Like a kid on Christmas morning.

"Yes?" Cisco beamed. "A date."

From behind the manga shelves, Bill, Audra's manager, popped up to watch us. Audra poked her head from around the same stand.

"If she doesn't say 'yes,' can we say yes for her?" Bill asked Audra.

"If she doesn't say 'yes,' I plan on making her do a signing every weekend. Somewhere new."

I took the sleeve from Cisco's coffee back, drew Bean nodding his head, and slid it back.

"Shh!" I said.

"Did she say yes?" Bill squealed, voice cracking.

Chapter Eleven

Change of luck?

Rina

Dodging Audra *and* Bill's questions was nothing short of torture. But apparently, leaving non-answers hanging in the air was just as bad. After paying for my manga, both Cisco and I left the store in furious shades of reds and pinks that were plain as day... even at night. I fumbled for my keys as Cisco walked me down the empty street. My beat to whipped cream and back sedan sat lonely under a street lamp.

"Is that whole situation going to be a problem?" Cisco dared to break the silence first, looking back at the store.

My phone vibrated with a text, and it didn't take a genius to figure out Audra already needed to pry more dirt from me.

"Audra? I mean..." Staring over the rim of my glasses, I watched the clouds move, waiting for the moon to make it's appearance.

He may have been blushing, but Cisco said, "She won't let you live anything down, will she?"

Judging by Cisco's laugh, my face was as easy to read as an open book. "I'm sorry," he said and tapped my shoulder.

"No! It's... fine. I don't... really date... I mean, I don't date. No, I do date. I haven't dated in... a long... *we are not* going on a date, though." Goodness, it was like I'd found my twin who happened to swear and not have pastries constantly on the mind.

My mouth and my brain do nothing but self-sabotage. It's the most joyous thing to ever happen... every time it happens. (It happens a lot.)

Cisco hesitated. His eyebrows knit together, and it made my heart twist. "Since... Caleb?"

Yes, since the utter disaster that was dating Caleb.

HOLD THE BANANA PUDDING!

"You know about that?" And with that squeal, my throat burned. Between puking my brains out and crying, my throat and head were a mess.

A little wobble in his voice crashed my heart straight into the pavement. "Well, it *was* a rumor... until now."

Fan-apple saucing-tastic.

We'd arrived at my car, but at what cost? Fat hot tears were forming behind my eyes, and the threat of driving and crying (once again, it wouldn't be the first time) was real. And, sure, my insides were empty (thanks to the amount of time spent in the bathroom at Book Smart), but I suspected my body would find something to puke up if I gave it a chance.

The questions were imminent. How could there not be? Audra had bombarded me after she first met Caleb. Surely, Cisco had pages of questions about that chapter of my life, too!

"I guess I can see it. Caleb's... like... human around you. Which no one ever suspected." Cisco's nervous laugh sent butterflies fluttering in all directions. "We were all formulating experiments to prove Caleb was either an artificial intelligence himself or an alien. I lean towards the alien theory."

I should have laughed. Cisco told a funny joke, and there was this awkward empty space in the joke's wake, but I couldn't quite muster the proper reaction. But my brain was stuck on a spin cycle with, 'People are talking about you.' Even if the talk is good, my brain freaks the strudel out.

"I should have kept my mouth shut. I'm sorry. It's not like everyone in the office is... actually, everyone is kind of talking about you. But not in a bad way. It's..." Spinning into my tunneling vision, Cisco held out a slightly lint-covered lollipop (lint on the wrapper) and a wide, maybe slightly unsure, grin. "Everyone loves you, Rina. They talk about you because you're... cool."

Nothing had ever sounded more like a lie in my entire life. There had been zero times I had ever been cool.

"It's true." The two words flowed like a melody, almost as if Cisco sang them, and he knelt on one knee. "You're incredible. Which, I guess, is embarrassing in its own way. Because everyone is talking about you... but it also means you're cool enough *to* talk about."

Even though my chest had lead weights on it, a new anxiety-induced tremor accompanying it, the weight lifted. Maybe grams (or ounces if I must use them) worth of the kilograms weighing my chest down, but it was something.

And all I could say was, "I'm not that lucky. In fact, usually, it's nothing but bad luck following me around." Especially after anything remotely good happens. Let's take this new shiny job of mine. Perfect fodder for terrible luck!

He held the lollipop further toward me, and I reluctantly took it, giving him the allowance to stand again. "What was so unlucky about today?" Cisco asked.

Heh... what indeed?

"I..." *Made a fool of myself? Am I going to be mocked mercilessly for the rest of my life? And let my best friend meet 'the cute guy at work.' Also... hadn't I lied to said cute boy about who I was? He'd been waiting to meet me at the convention. I...*

"For me, it couldn't have been better. Unless..." My doubt was reflected in Cisco's beautiful, large brown eyes. "...you can still back out of coming to the party. *I* am fully prepared to make a fool out of myself with my brother."

"No. Absolutely not!" Where did this resolve come from? I didn't have resolve with anything except telling Caleb no! "I'm... going." And apparently, continuing to lie to an entire family about dating their incredibly cute son.

My face had to be burning bright red again.

"You said you were unlucky." Holding his hand out, Cisco waited for the wrapper of the lollipop. "But *I* feel like the luckiest man around."

"Just wait..." I murmured.

"What?"

How had I let the words slip out? What is wrong with me? Had I not been pining over Cisco for... well, at maximum, a week... maybe a week and a half now?

Cisco stopped at my car, waiting by the driver's side door while I unlocked it with my key. I wasn't kidding when I said it was beaten to whipped cream and back. My car might resemble a wreck, and also, when I bought it, I couldn't afford anything automatic on her. Windows, locks, seat adjustment... everything was manual. As soon as the key returned from the lock, Cisco opened the door. "You never know. Maybe your luck is changing."

More weight lifted. "Good night," I said, sliding in behind the wheel. Carefully, I dropped the books I'd just bought on my pristinely clean passenger seat. I liked the thought my luck might be changing. Maybe I could even quell my hyperactive anxiety enough to ask Cisco on an actual date.

Instead of a send-off, he announced, "I like her!" Then stammered and slapped the roof of my car. "I like... the car. Right. Night!"

Cisco

Idiot. Dumbass. Stupid.

I like the car. What the hell was I thinking?

Everything else I'd said was true and suave, so why, in all the multiverses, did I say 'I like her' and mean the car?

Because... as I may have stated many times now... I'm. An. Idiot.

I sat in my car, parked up the street in the opposite direction from Rina's, and berated myself. Endlessly. Not like I was trying to be creepy and watch her leave... but more in the gentleman-y way of making sure she was safe as she left.

Until my phone pinged once.

Then twice.

Then, a bazillion times because Santiago hadn't started harassing me hardcore until I hadn't answered his tenth text. My unread messages went from 10 to 40 in no time. Then I refused to look after I muted his messages.

But by now, I had to appear utterly creepy to the outside observer. I started my POS, formerly a blue Civic (the Blue Beast... or sometimes just Beast), and pulled out of my parking spot. It wouldn't be that frightening to wave as I passed Rina's car, right?

As I pulled up, slowing so I could non-threateningly wave in her direction, Rina bashed her steering wheel. Gripping it, she shook it next, and tears would likely be next with her glassy eyes. What had I done? I hadn't meant to upset her...

She banged her head on the steering wheel, saw the Blue Beast and me, and I could practically hear her groan. Slowly, ever so slowly, her window lowered.

"Everything okay?" I called after I lowered Beast's passenger side window and heard the Beast's noisy purr and nothing else.

"Uh..." Rina's voice shuddered. "You wouldn't want to change your mind about my luck?"

Chapter Twelve

I rescind my statement

Rina

"This isn't an 'I told you so' moment," Cisco said from under the hood of my car. "Battery's not dead. It's trying to turn over. Something else is the issue, but I won't be able to figure it out tonight without more light."

"Pretty sure you're wrong," I huffed, banging my head on the arm I propped against the open hood.

"Not about the battery." Cisco beamed at me.

"About what kind of luck I have." Because not only was my apple strudel-ing car broken down—*again*—my screen lit with a warning. 5% charge left. "Thanks. I'll figure out a ride share…" And I shut the light off to conserve power.

"What about… Audra? Isn't Book Smart closed? She should be leaving soon."

Oh, if only that were a viable option.

"Audra lives there." I pointed at the building behind the row of shops. They built new apartments last year, and more people complained about the unsightly bland brick buildings, asking why anyone would want to live in them. Well, apparently, lots of people. Audra got one of the last apartments, a single bedroom, and shares it with her cousin, Wes many times. But the biggest problem was, "She doesn't have a car."

Cisco responded with a hiss. "Ok... well... what about...?"

"Bill owns a bike. And lives in the apartments above the sushi place down the street." It was a nice thought, though.

"Really?" And Cisco stared wistfully up the street at the sushi restaurant at the next stoplight. "That's a dream of mine. Extremely jealous now."

After Cisco slammed the hood shut, I sat on it, called up the first ride-share app on my phone, and scrolled, looking for a driver available that didn't set off any creep alarms.

"Where do you live?" he asked, sitting near me... though not too close. My heart hammered my chest, thankfully not as hard as earlier.

When asked that direct of a question, it's hard to dodge. "Uhhh, Hillshire?"

No other words were needed. If anyone spent any appreciable time in the area, they knew to avoid the Hillshire complex. It took up more space than any other complex. Also, it had more crime than any other area in Berkley's surrounding areas. No one could blame anyone for needing to live where rent was low to avoid being stuck in a confined space with their annoying brother. I had rent, student loans, and a paczki of a terrible time finding a job. FYI, I learned what a paczki was when working at VirTek, and a lovely woman on one of the security teams brought them in for Fat Tuesday. That's a whole other story.

"Hillshire?" Carefully, Cisco extracted a handkerchief from his back pocket and furiously rubbed away the grease.

He gave me more side-eye as I dropped the screen brightness to conserve battery power.

"Didn't I warn you about my luck?" Although, living in Hillshire had nothing to do with luck.

"I mean... I could give you a ride. And check if I have any extra pepper spray. Wasn't Hillshire on the news last week?"

I chewed on my lip, regretting leaving the lollipop in my car with the bag of books. I needed to chew on something!

Cisco's offer was so sweet, but..."It's probably really out of the way..."

Hopping off the hood, Cisco made a mad dash for my driver's side door. A dive in, and he had my books. "Hostages! Come on. It's too late to get a quick ride that far, anyway. And if you do, I'm not sure I trust whoever comes to whisk you away."

"You take a lot of hostages." I would have sounded grumpy, but it was cute how he held the books over his head even though I could still easily reach them.

"And I want to live out the whole fake-date trope with my family. You agreed... but I could give you another chance to opt-out." He held the passenger door of his car open again, waiting for me to lock my poor baby. Once settled, I needed to do one last thing.

> **Rina:** Car died. Leaving it in front of Book Smart until the morning. Getting a ride.

The text to Audra would cause more questions than answers, but that would have to wait because it also ate up the last of my phone's battery. Audra would know to call in my car, so I didn't get a ticket or towed.

Cisco pulled a dark pair of sunglasses from the center console and slid them on. "Let's roll."

"Can you see anything?"

"Not a thing." He dragged them down by the bridge, and I felt myself turn to mush at his grin. I clutched the bag of books in my lap to my chest. "But I look cool! Plus... you know... The Blues... never mind."

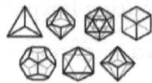

Cisco

Getting to Hillshire's complex was a pain, even in the middle of the night. I pretended not to get lost, but after making wrong turns left and right (heh, puns), Rina quietly provided directions.

When we passed under streetlights, I caught Rina biting her thumb ragged. However, words utterly failed me. Was there anything I could say that would turn Rina's mood around?

She caught my glance and buried her fists into the bag of books. "What was it you said about my luck?" Ah, the warble in her voice returned.

"Ok, well... how about something you can't contradict?" *Say it. Say it and be smooth, Cisco! You got this!* Pep talks rarely worked for me, but when a gorgeous woman is involved, I'll make every effort I can, no matter how corny. "My luck keeps getting better."

Rina scoffed. "You could be home right now if it weren't for me."

My phone vibrated against the middle of my freaking thigh, and extricating the damned thing required acrobatics while driving.

Santiago

Perfect timing. "Hey," I answered. "Can't talk."

Oh, I could transcribe what my brother complained about, mostly that I was still out when I should have been home helping our mama with dinner clean up, and so on...

"I'm driving Rina home. Her car broke down. BYE!" Blessedly stunned silence greeted me. Santiago would give me extra hell when he saw me next; fortunately, our schedules conflicted, and even when we were both home, we were both on opposite ends of the house, busy with our own projects. At this point, obviously, Santiago had been stalling so long on dishes that he'd run through every excuse in his book to pass the work off to me.

Rina pushed herself further into the seat when I caught her watching me. "Yes, m'lady?"

Suave. Right. That's me.

"How are you so confident?" She asked with the telltale blanched pallor she got when stressed out.

"You think I'm confident?" Apparently, I was that good at hiding my anxiety. Score, I guess?

I countered with a question of my own, "How do you keep from murdering Caleb when he opens his mouth?"

"I'm used to him. He's..."

"If you say 'he's not that bad,' I'm taking you back to work and ensuring you're not a Caleb built robo-.... uh, robo-scientist?" The joke might have fizzled out at the end, but Rina loosened her arms and jaw. So, I guess that was good enough to take the plunge and admit, "I'm not that confident, either."

Rina's eyebrows shot above her glasses.

I can't believe I had to defend my answer. "Really. I'm..." Sweating. Stomach twisting. "It's really hard to talk to a pretty girl... WOMAN! A PRETTY WOMAN." See... my brain hates me. If I were actually confident, I'd have asked Rina out already. On a proper date, not pretending to be my date for a family party.

And the chance to do that would have to wait. We pulled into Rina's complex and became distracted by her directing me toward a building. It became easier when she pointed to the one with flashing red and blue lights in front. I hadn't even stopped the car when she burst out, muttering to herself in the adorable pastry-infused swears and prayers that this had nothing to do with her apartment.

Before following, I dug out my pepper spray... not at all because the shadows caused by the police car's lights made mysterious figures appear and disappear. I caught her at the front door, which someone had propped open. Though past 10 pm, apartment doors were open, and people murmuring in the hallways. Rina stopped on the second floor, staring into an open apartment. Two officers were standing just over the threshold, taking notes.

Cautiously, I asked, "Rina?"

Her bag of books tumbled from her hands and spilled on the ground.

I didn't need to see the Lazy Bean pillow ripped open on the floor to know whose apartment I stared into. There was nothing to do now but wrap my arm around Rina's shoulders and run my hand up and down.

Her mouth opened to say something, but a strange, strangled noise came out instead of words.

Admitting defeat, I said, "I rescind my earlier statements on your luck."

A few tears dropped, wetting the front of Rina's blouse. Maybe my luck wasn't what I thought it was.

Chapter Thirteen

Grip like steel

Cisco

Rina stayed in a limbo state between panic and unnatural calm, answering the officers' questions but mostly going through the motions. Carnage in the form of Lazy Bean memorabilia, crafting supplies, stuffing, and feathers coated the main room. Her apartment was small but once well organized. Shelves stood in the far corner, cords littered where electronics had been hooked up.

She couldn't seem to walk but could list many big-ticket items she noticed were missing from her apartment just from standing on the threshold.

When the officers completed their questions, neighbors turned and slammed their doors as they returned to their lives. Rina stood silently in the middle of her home's remaining shambles, staring at a single spot on the floor near an empty entertainment stand.

This was the perfect time to cry. *I* wanted to cry. I'd never stepped foot in here before and felt utterly violated.

So, Rina's lack of tears made me a touch nervous about approaching her.

"Rina?" I sidled up to her, tucking my hair back before I inhaled quickly, trying to find the right words. Instead, I choked on it... as one does in the midst of a beautiful, emotionally overwhelmed woman of their dreams. When my choking subsided, I asked, "Maybe I can take you somewhere else. Audra might have room or...?"

A black framed picture lay cracked on the ground. The unfairly handsome guy from the convention at the Lazy Bean table stood with Rina, arms draped around each other. Obviously, not her boyfriend, since she confirmed herself that she hadn't dated anyone since Caleb.

"Do you have any family nearby?" I guessed. "A... brother?"

"Haru?" Her voice sounded far off.

"Okay, let's take you to Haru's place. Come on."

Prying the address from her, even shoving my phone loaded with the navigation app, took ages. I couldn't even be sure Rina put the correct address in until an agonizing half an hour later, holding her by the shoulders, we walked up to the almost pearlescent white brick building. All sleek glass and fancy-ass stone of some kind. This place was probably quadruple the rent Rina paid at Hillshire.

Takata, Haru

Rina's brother lived on the—*sigh*—fourth floor. I prayed this building had a working elevator. Steering and coaxing Rina up that many flights might be near impossible in her near-catatonic state.

I pushed the button labeled Takata and waited.

"Hello?" The half-asleep voice that greeted Cisco sounded unfairly hypnotic over the intercom. The Takata family must have fantastic genes—every one of them.

"H-hi? I'm a... friend of Rina's. She's with me... but... uh..."

"Just bring her up. The elevator is on the right. First door on the left."

Slipping my hand under Rina's arm made her jump, but when we locked eyes, she sucked in a long, shuddering breath and didn't seem to really see me. My palms (and kind of everywhere else) decided this was the best time to sweat profusely. But I still slipped my hand into Rina's. "Come on. Just a little further."

Pulling her through the door after it buzzed open was a slow process. Rina headed left when we needed to go right. She hit the wrong button on the elevator twice. We made two extra stops, and she mumbled about not having her resources finalized, almost as if she were at work.

Apartment 401's door swung open as we stepped off the elevator. The truly unfairly handsome guy I'd seen at the Bean table stood in the doorway, hair more rumpled and even more unfairly attractive than before.

At least he was her brother.

"Ok, Rin... come on," he said in a gentle, coaxing voice. Hey, I remember you. How'd the charm work out?"

My mouth flapped. *Well, damn it.* I'd hoped he wouldn't remember me. "Not... quite the way I'd expected."

Haru rustled his hair. Damn. I could go nowhere with this man even if Rina was with us. He might kill all the women with those looks. He might even kill me with those eyes and tousled hair.

"It's Rina, isn't it?" Haru guessed. "The woman you like."

I nodded dumbly.

"This," he waved at his sister's catatonic state and continued, "isn't because of that, though... right?"

Oh, I kind of wish Rina's current state had been entirely my intellect and charm. "Rina's car broke down, and I drove her home. But when we walked into her apartment, someone had broken into it."

Releasing the longest sigh imaginable, Haru led us into his apartment. And it took both of us to guide Rina to the couch.

"Rin?" Haru snapped in front of her eyes. "Nee-san? Ah...?" He glanced at me since Rina had my hand now in a death grip, and I was trying not to wince.

"We locked up as best we could." Ah, all I could do was grunt. "All the electronics were taken. Pillows ripped up and stuff."

"Her Lazy Bean stuff?" Haru asked, peering into his sister's glazed eyes.

"A few things were broken." For me, the sight was a gut punch. So much Lazy Bean stuff shredded and discarded like trash! Who could be such a monster?

"Yeah? I think this broke her." Haru snapped a few more times, but Rina didn't budge. "Do you mind staying a bit?"

"I'm not sure I can leave without a crowbar." Rina's grip increasingly tightened the longer we sat together.

"I'll put some tea on." Her brother gave me a wan smile. "I'm really sorry about this. Just give Rin a few minutes to loosen up, then you can head home."

Sure. Home. And leave Haru with nothing but my sweaty armpit stench and his practically catatonic sister to take care of.

I did eventually pry her hand out of mine, moving to wrap that arm around her shoulders. But her hand found my other hand fast and locked it in her shockingly vice-like grip.

"I don't want to go back," Rina mumbled after some time.

"I know," I said.

She turned, releasing my hand, and nearly gave me a heart attack as she lunged for me. And hugged me. Though I couldn't be sure she knew what was happening. A hearty sob traveled through her.

"Rina?" I asked. I knew it wasn't the time to ask her on a date. I'm not that heartless. Nor did I care if my shirt became soaked in tears. But I wasn't sure if she needed something because my shirt was getting wet and cold, and based on what happened earlier at Book Smart... I didn't peg Rina as a long-term hugger. Yet here she was, still hugging me. "Rina? I could grab a tissue. I can't give you my handkerchief. It's greasy..."

"Damn it!" Haru's abrupt entrance shook me.

And Rina still didn't move.

"What? This? I'm not..." *Oh, my God! This is it! Her brother had a murderous gleam in his eyes before and now I'm a dead man and...*

"She fell asleep!" Haru whined.

Chapter Fourteen

You'll know weird when you see it

Cisco

"Asleep?" I worried it would wake Rina after everything she'd been through but she didn't budge.

Also, drool covered my shirt. That would make sense.

"Look, man. I can help get her off you, and you can go home." With a rustle of his hair again, and a yawn, Haru added, "Thanks for bringing her by. I'll call a tow truck in the morning..."

"No." And there, my big dumb mouth went on again. "I'll swing by in the morning and see what I can do."

Taking a seat on a nearby sleek silver coffee table, Haru frowned at Rina. "As nice as that is, it won't win you a date with my sister. Not that I don't love her. She's just... really, *really*... not normal. I'm not sure there's a way to properly describe how shy Rina is. She doesn't do well with dating..."

"I got that." And I meant it, too. I understood. More importantl y... "But I want to help."

"You don't want to move, do you?" Haru sighed again, although it almost sounded a bit like a laugh. "She does anything weird; come wake me. I need some sleep."

"Weird?" I asked, now questioning every decision I'd made in the last five minutes.

"Not, like, to you. But when Rin's ultra stressed out... well, you'll know it when you see it." One final wave dimmed the lights in Haru's ginormous living room, and he muttered, "You've been warned."

Out of everything that happened, I balked. I couldn't help it. "You're really just going to leave your sister with me?" Who leaves their sister with a stranger in his living room?

I'm pretty sure I should have been offended when Haru let out a soft chuckle and said, "You aren't a guy I need to worry about."

See! Should have been offended... but it was hard to be too offended with Rina draped on my chest. Twisting like a pretzel, I reached behind my head, pulled a muscle, and gently pried her glasses off her face. Then, promptly, my shoulders regretted the awkward position. Rina, however, didn't stir at all. Laying my head on the back of the couch, I vowed to only close my eyes for a moment.

Sure... only a moment.

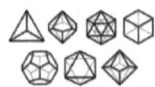

I woke up freezing my tuchus off to a blinding amount of light, and a disheveled Rina tripped over my foot, mumbling to herself. Somewhere, in the gleaming whites and light grays of Haru's apartment, she'd found a hair tie which, at most, encapsulated half her hair.

But her brother's kitchen? That was a real sight to see. Papers were taped everywhere—on cabinet doors, the vent hood for the stove, the dishwasher, the refrigerator, etc. The text was color-coded in vibrant markers and large print. I could read it from standing back several steps. Half asleep still, it took several minutes to figure out what I was looking at.

Computer code.

"Rina?" I asked, concern twisting my chest tight.

But she didn't answer. Rina kept writing and mumbling to herself, pushing up her glasses after she wrote a few lines of code.

I came up to Rina, passing my hand near her face. Even tried snapping. You know, not like a jerk, just trying to get her attention but she gave no reaction. As if I were invisible.

"Oh boy," I stumbled back, retreating to another part of the expansive apartment because this clearly wasn't good. Then, remembering that I had never been here before, I turned in wild circles. Where did Haru sleep?

I found a bathroom. Check.

What was that room? An office?

I found a closed door and bounced my fist off the wood. Not quite a knock, more of a frustrated thud. Should I even bother waking him?

The door opened and sent me stumbling back into an equally groggy Haru.

"She's doing it? God! Two hours of sleep? That's it?"

"Doing what exactly?" I followed Haru into the distressingly bright kitchen. My eyes adjusted, and I saw it was 2:30 am.

"During her master's work, it was the worst." Haru slapped lights on as he walked. "When Rina gets *hyper*-stressed, she enters *hyper*focus mode. The world falls away as she solves problems she *can* solve. She can't exactly solve someone breaking into her apartment, but..."

Pieces clicked together. "She's coding." I felt my own puzzle pieces coming together, too. "Like, old school pseudo-coding, but..."

"You work with her?"

"Yeah?" Shit. What had she told her family? Please tell me I didn't mess something up by telling Rina's brother something he didn't know. "Rina just started in our office," I squeaked.

"Rin on a project?"

Uhhh...? Should I say anything more? "She's barely started. I assume she's looked over the code a bit. They hired her to get the AI... well... working. The code is in serious shambles."

"Great," Haru moaned and started crumpling Rina's code to find coffee in a cabinet. "This,"—he waved at Rina mumbling and writing—"could last for days."

"Days?" I gaped at her, working while oblivious to us.

Haru continued making his coffee, dumping ground beans into the filter and slapping the switch to brew. "Yeah. Well, her car breaking down and her apartment broken into? Days sound about right. She won't eat and she'll fall asleep at her desk... days of this. Rina doesn't do well with stress."

If anything could be considered overwhelming, this was it. I... was officially getting myself in over my head.

The more I stared at the colorful code littering Haru's wall, the more I recognized something I didn't think would be so alluring.

Rina coded beautifully.

And I never thought that would be such a huge turn-on.

"Rina?" I crossed the kitchen, leaning down to try to catch her eye.

"It all stems from the beginning. There's no..."

As slowly as possible, I covered her hand with mine. "What can I do?"

Haru chuckled. "I don't suggest diving into this. You're already in too deep for the normal person. I got this."

Leaving didn't sit right with me. I glanced around at the sheets and back at Rina. She numbered them. Clever. So, I started pulling them down in order.

"I'm serious. You're not dealing with normal here, and that's saying something. Rina doesn't attract normal very often."

Did Haru consider me normal?

Haru continued, "I don't think you know what you're getting into, and you seem like a nice enough guy."

Gathering the sheets still, pulling the tape off the backs so they didn't stick together, I raced around the kitchen. "I'll take Rina to the office. She'll have more space to work, and you can sleep."

Haru grabbed the pot and considered a mug but chose a straw instead. Reaching into another cabinet, Haru produced a sticky note and pen, then scrawled a few phone numbers. "My number. Audra's number. Give me yours. I'll send breakfast up to Infinite in a few hours. And remember, I tried to warn you." Haru took a long drag on the coffee and added, "Audra will need updates. I charged Rina's phone, and Audra was blowing it up last I checked."

"Is that drool?" Mandy wiped at the corner of my mouth. Had I fallen asleep making coffee again?

Third cup... no fourth? The coffee wasn't working. I needed sleep. "What time is it?" I asked since the clock on the opposite wall of the breakroom kept wavering in and out of focus.

"Were you working all night again? You can't keep up with Caleb, but that's fine. He's a robot! Stop trying to kill yourself..." Mandy's perkiness couldn't infiltrate my sleep-deprived state.

I poured and missed my coffee cup, so Mandy snatched the pot and poured it for me. "Okay, this is bad, even for you. I'll cover for you. Go home and get some sleep. Or is Santiago..."

"No... well, yes, Santiago was being his usual *chipper* self." But fortunately, the texts had stopped. "But nah, I'm good. I'll sleep here. I just ended up driving Rina home."

Coffee overflowed like a brown waterfall over the top of my mug and burned Mandy's fingers. "You... what?"

"Heh, yeah. It sounds more romantic than it was." I took the mug, dumped half into the sink, and grabbed six packets of sugar and cream.

Mandy, in her impeccable skirt suit and silk shirt, heels clicking on the tile floor when she came to meet me at the sink, practically screamed, "You're not the king of romance. So, tell me what happened!"

"That's hurtful. Son of a biscuit!" I turned to toss the empty sugar packets in the garbage, and there was Caleb, practically on top of me.

He raised one eyebrow over his punchably chic frames and took the coffeepot—literally, the whole coffee pot. "Clean up your mess, Cisco."

Mandy wheeled on me. "I heard Rina swear like that. Or not swear... oh, my God! You spent the night with her."

"I did," I said, tossing a kitchen towel on the coffee but lacking the energy reserves to actually wipe it up. "But it's not what you think."

Mandy followed me down the hallway, but I kept walking to Rina's instead of turning for my office. Rina spent considerable time taping the papers from Haru's (and a whole boatload more) all around her office. It started from next to the doorway, stretching in long lines from as high as she could reach down to her knee level. Hours' worth of writing became a new wallpaper that touched anything close to the wall. Her whiteboard on wheels, monitors... anything. At the center of the room, Rina lay draped on her desk, asleep again. I'd found a rolling cart, snagged my laptop from my office, and began the arduous task of transferring all of Rina's current pseudocode.

"What the heck is all this?" Mandy squinted at the code.

"This is..." My brain stalled for a moment until I remembered, "A.R.T.I."

"Artie?" she asked.

"Augmented Reality... uh.... I don't remember the rest. Rina wrote it."

"Wrote the name or the code?" Tiptoeing into the room to not wake Rina, Mandy checked out some of the early code.

After I chugged my coffee, I answered, "Yes."

"Yes?"

"All of it. Or A.R.T.I.'s skeleton." I couldn't work at the same frantic pace Rina did. "Like seriously bare-bones fixes for our existing code. But I think what she wrote will get it up and running. There are bits of the existing code printed and taped in there." Not that I could see that right now. My vision went double a while ago. Rina's large print was the only thing that saved me when I began inputting the code into a new file. Rina never even noticed. She just kept working and mumbling.

"How? Why? This isn't a date, Cisco. You're supposed to take a girl out for dinner and..." Mandy whispered, mouth agape while she walked the office.

"I know that!" I didn't need any help to kick myself for not actually asking Rina out yet. "We have a fake date tomorrow... if we can break this evil spell."

Returning to the door and pushing me—which rolled me—into the hallway, Mandy growled, "You really need to catch me up on what happened last night."

"Sure. Then catnap, and I'll need you to cover for me."

Mandy realized our voices probably carried into Rina's office, so she shuffled over and closed the door. "I said I would so you could get sleep."

"I'm not going to sleep long. I need to see a bookstore about a car."

"Honey," Mandy grabbed me by the shoulders, stared into my dead tired soul, and said, "What. The. Hell. Happened. Last. Night?"

Chapter Fifteen

It works? It works!

Cisco

"What is so important that you made me drive into work at 7:14 in the God-forsaken morning on a *freaking* Saturday?" Mandy pinched my arm and slammed an extra large iced coffee beside my hand.

I chewed my lips and stared at the screen in Test Lab #1, the biggest of the labs with the biggest screen. I needed everything large and questioned if I was hallucinating or not.

"Is that what I think it is?" I asked, pointing at a blinking cursor on the screen. It kept up a steady pace after it had typed an answer.

Mandy squinted at the screen. She'd thrown her long hair into a tight bun. Clearly, the woman had been somewhere last night, maybe a club, since she sported clothes I'd seen her in the night before when she dropped by to invite me... somewhere. God, every time I lifted my eyelids, it got more difficult. That was last night, right? Mandy asked me... oh, forget trying to remember!

She must have spent the night not at home. But Mandy refused to go anywhere without makeup and had thrown on deep red lipstick and sunglasses to give the illusion she wasn't doing the walk of shame. "Who's AI are you running? You trying to…"

"Ours." I rubbed my eyes again.

"Ours doesn't work." Mandy reminded me.

"Rina's fixes…"

Mandy didn't let me finish. "It's still erroring out."

"Yes, but it's running. It's never gotten this far before. A.R.T.I. is, for all intents and purposes, actually… working. Unless I'm completely mistaken."

Mandy's eyes focused and unfocused, and she typed, and… her quiet was lulling me to sleep.

"Holy crap," Mandy beamed, shaking me until I jolted upright.

"What?" I gathered myself after a moment of peaceful, almost escape to dreamland.

"The AI works?" Caleb asked from the door.

I knew I was hallucinating now because when I turned around, Caleb actually… smiled.

Or this was a nightmare. Probably a nightmare.

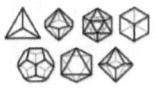

Rina

Something radiated warmth next to my hand. And stale coffee wafted around my head like a buzzing fly. I sat up and scratched the thick mop of hair I'd apparently half pulled into a messy bun at some point. Yawning was more difficult than it should be. Something stuck to my face. I pulled a sticky note from my cheek and looked around.

Huh...

That was a lot of paper covering my office. Every inch of space. Some overlapping.

Oops.

I reached for the coffee...

Hang on, one frittering minute. I didn't remember making coffee.

What the applesauce day was it?

"Congratulations are in order," Caleb said from behind me, studying the first papers on the wall next to the door.

"Huh?"

"Normally, I wouldn't be so cavalier about you usurping one of my engineers, but you always were efficient. Especially during your masters." A gentle smile crossed Caleb's lips.

"Usurp?" I worried this was a weird dream. I had zero recollection of anything. My brain haze bothered me, too. This only happened when...

Caleb sat on the edge of my desk. "Reyes isn't usually such a diligent worker, either. But getting the code viable in such a short time... I'm pleasantly surprised he did so well."

"What day is it?" I finally asked and took a gulp of stale coffee, cream, and... caramel. Just the way I like it. Caleb's grin grew, and I... was that warmth in his smile? No... that's impossible.

"Saturday." He crossed his hands in his lap. "You've been in one of your... work modes."

Saturday? How was it Saturday? *Think, Rina, think!* What was the last thing that happened?

...

Book Smart. New manga and graphic novel haul. That was... Thursday?

My stomach realized before me.

Cisco Reyes. In Book Smart.

Holding his arm.

Kissing his cheek.

Snatching a stack of paper off my desk, I buried my face and blocked the potential vomit that threatened to make a sudden appearance. "Saturday? I... two days?"

Two days of...

"My car!" I squealed. "My... oh... apartment."

I would have rather stayed in the trance of working.

Sniff.

Oh, goodness, I needed a shower too!

"Wait," I realized incredibly slowly. "I didn't usurp anyone."

"Reyes has been working on your code for days."

"No, he hasn't," I insisted.

"Rina," Caleb turned me to face him, even as I curled into a tight ball on the desk chair. Bending, Caleb crouched so I could look him in the eye. "He took my time on our infrastructure from me. I *should* have written him up when I got the alert... but it worked."

I shoved Caleb off me, letting the paper rain onto the floor. "What worked?"

"The fixes for the AI. It's run more than any other engineer we had that's worked on it. I'm not surprised. You're..."

"This isn't in the code. It's all just theoretical." When I got into my hyperfocus mode... things got hazy, sure, but also, I didn't type. I wrote everything by hand. That's how it always went.

"Reyes abandoned his project and has been working with you for the last couple of days. Excellent work, Rin."

I should have caught it. Thinking back, I can't believe I was so blind... or deaf.

"He has?"

Cisco

"How is she?" Haru had kept close tabs on his sister. Between trying to keep up with her coding, fixing her car, cat naps, and fielding calls and texts from Audra and Haru, I had zero time to do anything Caleb assigned. I'd barely eaten, either. I had to wonder what the hell Haru did for a living. He seemed to be up at all hours, half asleep, but always ready to do some random thing for Rina. Send her food, clean her apartment, fix her door, etc.

Two days of not being home, not showering, and barely any sleep left me only slightly more energetic than a zombie. I moved around the silent hallways of Infinite, grateful for the weekend's emptiness.

"Rina was sleeping last time I checked on her," I said and heard Haru shuffling around wherever he was. "Thanks for sending breakfast again today, or was that..."

"Dinner. Rina's got you working hard. Not sure what you think you're getting out of this man. You seem far too cool for my sister. And I already said..."

Because I was sleep-deprived, and not because I'd completely lost the filter between my mouth and brain, I replied, "Your sister seems far too cool for me. And I'm not doing it for anything. I like Rina. End of story. I don't mind helping."

"I know I keep repeating it. I just worry you'll get frustrated with my sister. Rina's pretty decent as sisters go. But she's oblivious. I'm kind of rooting for you, but..."

I'd found my way back to Rina's office, the door open and voices coming from inside, and stopped dead in my tracks.

"Dr. Wellington is more than impressed. He wants to showcase it to investors when you get it working to full capacity. Start the learning process and such." Caleb's *dulcet* voice carried into the hallway.

"What? NO! This isn't... you're..."

"Breathe, Rin."

My hand dragged along my face. *Rin? Caleb? Shit!!!!*

All I had to do was walk another pace, and I could see Caleb standing close enough to Rina to touch her cheek.

No... correction. Caleb *was* touching her cheek.

"How about dinner tonight? I can make reservations for Cuisine D'Amour. 7pm? We can celebrate."

My stomach flip-flopped, like a fish out of water, as I backed away from the door.

Haru asked, "Cisco? Are you still there? Everything okay, bro?"

"Uh?" My mouth dried and could probably be used as sandpaper. "Yeah. No. Rina's fine. She's talking to our boss. I... I gotta go."

As soon as I hung up on Haru, a text came through.

> **Santiago:** Can't wait to see tu mamacita tonight.

Well... shit.

Chapter Sixteen

Cinderella time

Rina

"Dinner?" Apparently, my brain and my mouth weren't meeting in the middle. I kind of saw it coming, but when Caleb asked, it still hit me like a train.

Caleb's mouth quirked up. "Yes. I'd like to..."

"Saturday? Saturday? Something... happening on Saturday...?" I interrupted again in a panicked whisper. "I can't! I have plans."

Rarely have I caught Caleb off guard. "Do you have a date?" he asked.

"No. Yes. Kind of. I don't know." This time, the anxiety didn't make me nauseated. It just wound me tight, like I might snap. "Oh... cinnamon buns!"

And I might have been hyperventilating. Just a little.

How was I going to get anywhere? My car broke down. I didn't know anything like where Cisco lived or the party's time. I was — for lack of a better word — screwed.

Cisco

I found myself back at Test Lab #1, somehow in less pain than I expected from all the kicking I did to myself.

I hadn't lied to Haru. I wasn't helping Rina to get anything from her. But all the excitement over having her with me at the party had evaporated.

"Who died?" Mandy had taken over my seat, somehow still wearing her sunglasses but also fiddling with A.R.T.I. at the same time.

"My social life?"

Mandy giggled, even if it caused a wince. She didn't hear my voice crack. If she had, she wouldn't have joked, "That's already dead because you never come out with me when I invite you."

What little hope burning inside me fizzled. "We don't frequent the same places." Was I sulking? Yes. "And you go out once a month, max."

"I tell you about once a month. I go out... that's neither here nor there." Mandy seemed to catch on slowly that I was shutting down and packing up to go home. "Wait. What happened?"

What else was there to say other than, "Caleb asked Rina out." I had been MIA for days now and in desperate need of a shower.

"Ok... and?" Mandy slapped my hand when I tried to close the laptop.

"He asked her out, Mandy." I jammed a notebook into my bag. "For tonight." *Don't make me say it out loud! You're one of my best friends.*

"Your mom's party? OH!" The last exclamation must have hurt because Mandy winced again and grabbed her sunglasses, steadying the room.

"It's not a big deal. I'm going to get some sleep before the tortuosity begins." I tossed the extra large soda cups and takeout containers in the trash and continued the barrage, kicking myself all the way back to my office and then my car.

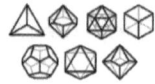

Rina

Why? Why, why, why, why, why?

I. Am. So. Dumb.

Caleb seemed as nonplussed as ever, but how could I miss it?

"Think about it. I'm... open," Caleb said, running his hand up my arm just before he walked out.

But now I sat in my office, covered in crazy-person papers, and sulked. I'd not only royally applesauced up, but I had no way to fix it.

"Caleb," Mandy snapped on her way up the hallway. Or maybe she did? I could have been hallucinating. Dreaming that someone else was in Infinite that could help. Wouldn't that be... "Rina! Oh, thank... holy crap!" She lifted some oversized sunglasses and squinted. "Shower. That's for sure. And clean clothes. I probably have something in my desk. Makeup. We can do this before the party."

Party?

I bolted upright. "Mandy?" I was so ecstatic I could cry. I did cry. "Oh, I need a ride and... and... I need to know where Cisco lives..."

Caleb's rather on-brand derisive laugh came from the hallway. If he said anything, we didn't hear it. I slammed the door to block out any further interruptions and continued, "And I need..."

Mandy slid the dimmer for my office lights down and smiled without needing to squint. "You don't know?"

"Know what?" The urge to hurl returned with a fierce vengeance.

"Where to begin?" Mandy lifted her sunglasses just enough to take in my office. "Well, Cisco fixed your car. He drove it here and left it in the parking space beside his. And other than that... I don't think he's really left your side for over two days. He took you to your brother's place after the apartment break-in. Fed you. Took all your code and dropped it into a new file, and got A.R.T.I. running. Like we're talking this is the first time Cisco has left your side."

"Is he still here?" I secretly prayed I could fix this without too much trouble.

Mandy gave me a slow headshake. "But!" she exclaimed brightly, maybe too brightly even for her. "We have work to do and probably a lot less time than we think to do it in."

I held up a finger. "I don't share makeup. That's disgusting. Too many germs and..."

"Relax!" Mandy snapped. "Can we please just do the magical fairy thing and make you beautiful?"

"I am beautiful," I said with a pout.

"True that, sister. But you know... let's make you look less like a crazy person. Because you're currently giving off crazy person vibes."

Currently I had no leg to stand on. Hyperfocus mode ended in the most brutal of manners. Mandy's grimace said it all. Crazy person standing right in front of her. "Then we'll send you to the most excruciating ball imaginable and please make this a happy ending for Cisco and you. You two are too cute."

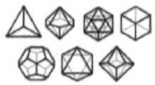

Cisco

The nap was a no-go the second I walked into my parents' house. Santiago's stupidly charming smirk from the kitchen was all I needed. Mamá rushed me around, finishing last-minute decorations. She had me lugging *even more chairs* from the garage and basement and hanging more streamers and balloons than had any right fitting on the wall.

Even after several cousins arrived, I was still hard at work while Santiago waved his second and then third beer at me.

"Where's your princesa, hermano?" Santiago grinned.

Knife twisting deeper.

"Rina is finishing a..."

The doorbell interrupted me. Mamá waved me to the door, mumbling who that could be. The family never rang the doorbell; instead, they just walked in.

I opened the door, still distracted by Santiago's tipsy laugh, and said, "Great. Santiago, did you have a date...?"

"Cisco?"

I started at my name coming from the girl standing there, sounding anxious. Familiarly anxious. Agnoizingly familiarly anxious.

It took a long moment of looking over the girl to realize she was Rina, wearing a cute green dress that flared at the bottom, her thick glasses framed by bouncy black curls, blushed cheeks, and bright red lips.

My mouth became a desert. I blinked over and over at Rina because seeing her dressed like this and on my parents' doorstep was more likely a hallucination than anything.

Rina

I clutched the small box of fresh mochi, which had been literally the only thing my brain could think to stop and get. Applesaucing brain. It was panic, and now I looked at it... BUT I couldn't show up empty-handed. I clearly had not thought it through. Even looking just past Cisco, the living room seemed packed, and I could hear more people beyond there in the house.

"Rina?" he choked on my name.

The pitiful pack of pink and white mochi—six in total—would not cut it. But I couldn't exactly leave, especially with Cisco staring at me.

"How did you—No, better question, aren't you—" Cisco lowered his voice for the next part. "—late for your date with Caleb?"

"Date?" That knocked a whole new set of worries into my brain. "No. There was no date. Why..." Mother flipping pancakes. I wanted to die. I tried to double over because my stomach roiled, except I felt the short skirt riding up. "There... is..." My body really was about to betray me. Bile rose in my throat. "There..."

"Turn," Cisco gently made me face the rose bushes in the front yard. "Are you gonna throw up?"

Most definitely, I thought. I would have shaken my head, but even the thought nauseated me. The most I could do was take out my phone and, still crouched, tap out a message.

> **Rina:** Mandy told me what you did. I really can't thank you enough.

My thumb hovered over the send button. There was more I wanted to say, but the words stuck like glue in my brain and refused to make their way out. Eventually, I hit send through the protests of my stomach and nerves.

"Hey, it's.... Nothing," Cisco's warm voice... I could hear the smile even though I absolutely couldn't look him in the eye.

Someone started saying something in Spanish in the house, but I couldn't tell what. Cisco answered back in only a series of frustrated grunts, but it was the distraction I needed to type the next text and hit send.

> **Rina:** If I had the nerve, I would have asked you on an actual date, not just pretending to be your girlfriend today.

The ding of the text, Cisco's hand tightening on my arm. I swore I could feel his breath stop. And the butterflies taking over my stomach? They all fluttered away.

Standing back up, I felt like I had dragged Cisco's hand. He blinked at his phone, then at me when I gathered the surging bits of courage.

"Do... do you think..." For all the courage I thought I mustered, I tripped over every word. "I mean... would you want to go... on... a... date?"

Cisco stared, stuck in a loop, but he eventually answered with a silent nod.

Clutching even harder, probably cracking the plastic case, I leaned closer. After I pecked Cisco's cheek and realized that I was wearing more makeup than usual, including lipstick.

"Aye? Panchito?" an older woman called, then immediately gasped.

This propelled Cisco. "Mamá? Ah...?" I couldn't wipe his cheek without it looking... weird. Oh, banana pancakes, there was nothing I could do that wouldn't look out of place and... like... his girlfriend. "Meet.... Rina. My..." Cisco gave me a questioning look before continuing, "...girlfriend?" Though he added in a low whisper, "Are you still going to throw up?"

"Very possibly," I answered back.

"You didn't throw up asking..." He thought better of what to say and changed course. "You didn't throw up a moment ago."

"It was close." The box of mochi in my hand, the plastic crushed by my applesaucing anxiety, could not get hidden fast enough.

"Is that... Did you bring a desert...?" Cisco's sweet grin should have eased the pressure on my stomach.

It didn't. I turned back to the bush just to be safe.

Chapter Seventeen

Fish out of water

Mandy

"I don't get it."

Heading to a comic book store was decidedly *not* what I wanted to do on a Saturday afternoon. An important point of fact: I have never stepped foot in a comic book store. Generally, my social life comprised girls' nights at the club twice, thrice... maybe a few more times than that a month with a few university friends still living in the Berkley area. There was also my anti-social life,—going out to forget things— but I didn't tend to talk about that much. Of my few university friends, only a couple were still single. Currently, that amounted to... two friends... soon to be one. We saw each wedding coming the week they'd started dating their significant others, and I knew each were the luckiest girls in the world.

Monica's bachelorette party loomed, and I couldn't stop thinking about how she'd found her ideal girlfriend (soon-to-be wife)—a girl who happened to be her best friend.

Even Cisco and Rina's budding romance almost seemed like something one might see in a cheesy teen drama.

My heart screamed to know every detail but also ached to hide and silently watch their adorable, insanely geeky flirting.

I wanted that so badly for myself.

Though, for me, I preferred less geeky and more straightforward flirting.

Except, so far that has not worked out for me in the last few months. Or years. It hasn't even worked that well during the last decade.

Lately, all I could seem to manage were one-night stands...

So, since my attempts were futile, I lived vicariously through Cisco's stories. And during those, he'd convinced me to attend a drop-in dragon session—or something like that—just to get more second-hand adorable romance action. Not that Cisco provided any actual action.

"You play like every other week. You literally played last week. So... what is this again?" With one hand, I smoothed a curl of chestnut hair over my shoulder and clutched the paper coffee cup in my other. The neon sign and posters in the window up the street made me realize how overdressed I was, even in plain black jeans and a ribbed t-shirt.

"So, there's this DM..." Cisco started and lost me already.

"What's a DM?" I asked.

He made a sharp clicking sound with his tongue and responded with his own scathing question, "Did you listen at all when I explained this to you yesterday? Profusely explained. Because I *asked* you to understand what you were getting yourself into before we got here."

I.... Definitely did not listen well enough, obviously. I'd been trying to imagine Cisco sweetly rubbing circles on Rina's back, praying she wouldn't throw up after he'd given his mom the mochi she'd brought (even if the party happened weeks earlier). From the story he'd told a couple of weeks ago, Cisco's mother fussed over Rina, calling her beautiful in various forms. All while his annoying brother, Santiago, sulked or tried to interject how much he'd *known* their mother would adore her when he'd met Rina at the bookstore.

But the actual *act* of trying the mochi was when Cisco's own sunny side became brighter than the sun.

He thought the world of Rina, and I could tell just by how his eyes lit up at the mere mention of her name, let alone the adorable things she did.

"My mom flipped because Rina brought a gift at all."

"But...?" Mandy had kept prompting him to get more information.

"But, biting into the actual mochi...? Mami... tried."

"Have you had mochi?" Mandy had. The gummy, chewy texture wasn't everyone's preference.

"Of course!" Cisco said, practically offended. "What kind of weeb do you think you're talking to? Mamá patted Rina's cheek and still kept calling her princesa. So... I think she's planning our wedding as we speak. And I think she kept the box label in her scrapbook."

And from there, in a few short weeks, Cisco and Rina were full of stinking adorable stories.

"Dungeon. Master." Cisco closed his eyes while he walked, trying to keep himself calm. "He's going to lead us through the story, give us the setting and monsters, and so on."

"Right." I had no idea what Cisco was saying. But how could it be more complex than working at Infinite Labs and *not* murdering Caleb on a daily basis? We were drawing closer to the store, so I asked again, "Why isn't this a cute date with Rina?"

"She's side hustling today. She's sketching at an event because she found a new apartment. Rent is almost double what she had been paying."

"Wait." I did the math. Cisco was a few years younger, but he made a livable wage. And from what I gleaned from his stories, the last place Rina lived in was dirt cheap. "Shouldn't her salary at Infinite be more than enough...?"

"Haru and I tried to tell Rina, but she wants to do this alone. I think she's trying to buy new equipment before the insurance check clears, and her bank account definitely won't allow for that right now."

They'd meandered all the way down the street and now stood in front of the poster-covered door. A mishmash of posters never looked good, but this had a certain charm.

"Ok! Quick charisma check." Cisco held the door closed so I couldn't open it and fiddled with his bag with his other hand.

"Excuse me?" I coughed on the coffee. "I have a thousand percent more charisma..."

"My hair beats yours, hands down." True enough. Some days, the slight natural curl of Cisco's hair had beat out mine. Few guys had such stunning hair as Cisco. "My charisma is literally off the charts."

"Hair and charisma are not the same..." I bit my tongue. "What did you want to say?"

"Don't embarrass me. I have been waiting for *literally* ever for Arcane to open a one-shot session and have room to get me in. None of my party is here. Rumor is he's super nice to new players, but that doesn't mean..."

"Why are you worried about *me* embarrassing *you*?" I might have snapped a little.

Cisco pointed to his shirt (with some alien on it and a joke I didn't get) and his bag (covered in patches from shows and anime I definitely did not recognize) and... I got the picture. I was the fish out of water.

"Noted." Waving at his hand, I asked, "Can we please go inside before I change my mind and go home?"

Chapter Eighteen

Surprise geeky twins

Cisco

Opening the door to Tome Raiders (literally the coolest name for a comic book shop *ever*)... well, it should have happened easier. I stood there, hand on the handle, waiting like something magical or religious would happen.

Mandy's impatience won out, and she snatched the handle and slammed open the door, grumbling about who would embarrass whom here.

I've been to comic shops. Many in my time. Tome Raiders was like most. Comics lining the walls on shelves, comic boxes stacked with plastic sleeves sticking up. Brightly painted walls peeked through the thin gaps between the comics and shelves. But above the shelves of collector's figures swirled dragons, superheroes, and icons from the biggest and smallest sci-fi and fantasy shows. It was a true nerd haven.

And I'm man enough to admit that I squeaked from pure, unadulterated joy.

Also, I'm man enough to admit that I couldn't say anything for a full minute after we walked in.

Because there, standing in front of the counter, was Arcane himself. Tall, slender, fitted button-down shirt and scarf wrapped around his neck. Purposely messy dark blonde hair combed forward, laying partially across clear plastic framed glasses. Arcane's reputation grew on social media because of his funny videos about tabletop RPG life. The guy was a legend, and I was standing at the entrance of his incredible store, unable to move, or speak...

"Hey! Welcome! Are you here for...?" Arcane pointed at a table near the counter, or rather two folding tables shoved together but covered in a tablecloth that looked like grass, mountains, and all kinds of other terrains.

"I... I..." My mouth flapped. God, I wish Rina was here to help me out. Her nerves, coupled with mine, would make the perfect excuse for neither of us to talk, and we could run and hide together. Or I could make excuses because she'd probably be such a big fan of Arcane as well and...

I couldn't do this. Going on dates with Rina was one thing... but this had been a very different kind of dream about to come true, and my ability to self-sabotage was surprisingly as high as Rina's self-sabotage level!

"Ignore him. Yeah, we're here for your... game?" Mandy finished for me.

Arcane lit up, and I should have fainted. I did feel lightheaded, so it wasn't out of the realm of possibilities.

"Join us! Come on!" Arcane bounced over to us and guided us in. "You are... wait, let me guess! You're..."

"Cis...Cisco... Reyes?" Then I remembered I would have given Arcane my character handle, "I mean..."

"I remember you! You always have the best comebacks on my videos!" And Arcane grabbed my shoulders in one swoop and hugged me. "I can't wait to see your character! I gotta guess... wait... you told me the name but not the class or species... ugh... I don't want to assume, but... halfling? No! Gnome! Wait... I'm going back to my first guess... halfling!"

I might have fallen over if Arcane weren't holding my shoulders. *He knows my species!*

"We've got some other new players already here," Arcane continued on as if I were acting like a totally normal person. "And I'm waiting for my cousin to run the register and another player..."

Arcane's voice trailed off. I heard noises, but the words were bleeding together, and I couldn't focus. I sat down with two other players. Mandy sat beside me, and Arcane kept going about something my brain could not comprehend.

I heard nothing until a bell dinged and Mandy exclaimed, "Rina?"

"Apple fritters!"

Uh? Apple fritters did not compute. That was Rina's thing... and Mandy shouted her name, but... Rina was busy with her side hustle.

"You cannot run away from your boyfriend!" Audra laughed and swiveled Rina around to face us again.

"I'm running away from Wes," Rina ground out the words. "Not Cisco."

And like that, I had sudden clarity. "Rina?" I asked.

She cradled her bag and had all but abandoned her rolling suitcase of art supplies for Audra to lug.

"No!" Arcane — Wes, apparently — gasped. "No! This is *him*? The fabled boyfriend!" And I noted Arcane's voice took on a squeaky quality.

All of a sudden, Arcane was all squeals, Audra gleamed, and Mandy cackled.

"Pretty work boy plays D&D, and no one told me?" Audra sauntered by, ruffling my hair while dragging Rina with her.

"It didn't come up," Rina huffed, still trying to break free. "I didn't know."

"I wish it had come up. You..." I lowered my voice, which was stupid considering how small the shop was, "You *know* Arcane?"

"OH!" Audra exclaimed, "he's fanboying still, isn't he?"

"He'll get over it soon," Arcane waved the worry away.

"How?" I wondered, well aware that eyes were on us, including strangers sitting at the table impatiently waiting for the game to start.

"Uh... Hi, Mandy." Rina leaned to the side, waving. "Wes is Audra's cousin. We all went to school together."

Ah, the manly squeak escaped again. Though... there was more than one. *I* made one, but apparently, Arcane did as well.

"No one told me *the boyfriend* had such fabulous hair and..." Arcane squealed.

"You can't be in love with him," Audra sighed, trying to ward away a headache by pinching the bridge of her nose. "You have a fiancé and..."

"He's taken," Mandy finished, winking at Rina.

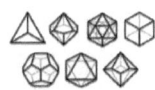

Audra

Holy.

Crap.

Mandy, Cisco, and Rina's friend was hot. Like 'walking down the street, make people turn their heads' hot. But I had to keep my head since Rina was utterly incapable. The girl went into a tailspin with all the stress of the last few seconds, and someone had to keep her head cool in the face of such hotness. And, like usual, that person was me.

Don't get me wrong, Cisco tried. "Why didn't you tell me?" But he was too squeaky.

"Bigger question," I added, seeing the flight response starting in Rina with how rigid she became. "Why didn't you tell *me* lover boy was into the dragon?"

Pulling art supplies and character cards she'd made in the past, then setting them carefully on little plastic displays, Rina said, "Never came up."

"How—in all the unearthly amount of geekery—did it not come up?" I continued, which let me catch a glimpse of their friend, Mandy's, sweet smile.

Mandy offered, "I think we know what they were doing instead," with a salacious eyebrow waggle.

There it was! Rina's tailspin went into a total dive bomb. And she'd turned bright red. Carefully pulling character sheets off the furthest table for their game, Rina climbed up and... did not grace us with a table dance. What is wrong with my bestie? Did I teach her nothing? Apparently not, because she was pulling comics off the top wall-mounted rack. "I think a dragon would look great..."

"What *are* you doing here?" Mandy asked. "And there are plenty of dragons."

"Sometimes I do character sketch commissions at the games. Or cons. Also, Audra, there are never enough dragons." From thin air,

Rina produced a pencil, committing to the idea of a dragon painted on the wall between two legendary superheroes.

I would say, "I'm not sure we need another..." but Wes squealed again. An ear-splittingly loud and boisterous squeal.

Cousin of the year ran over and snatched Rina's legs, pulled her carefully off the table, and set my bestie on the floor. "Oh! Girl! I'm so proud of you. And a bard, too?"

Cisco sat, mouth flapping wildly, random sounds occasionally escaping until he made one word, "How?"

But with Wes clasping Rina's shoulder and holding her close, he turned towards Cisco, a huge smile spread across Cisco's face, infectious to all but the two strangers sitting at the table. One of said strangers, with his dirty-ass feet kicked up on the table, "Can we freaking start already? Or do we need to keep watching the lamest tween drama in existence?"

Chapter Nineteen

A bard, a cleric, and a druid band together

Cisco

"Gonna be really hard to get started with *someone* not having a character," Audra said from behind me, paper rustling as she flipped through a comic.

Twisting around, my mouth returned to flapping. "What? Is your family full of mind readers?"

"Puh-lease!" Audra didn't bother putting down the latest in horror comics, a zombie staring back at me. "Someone like... *her* has never played before. Rin-rin! Where's your binder!"

I turned again to find Rina had somehow slipped from Arcane's grasp and was back on the table, stress-drawing a dragon on the wall. "Front pocket. Against the marker case."

Audra took the seat next to Mandy with a huff.

"Come on! Why can't we start already?" the guy across from me snapped. He looked similar to Arcane, with mussed brown hair and glasses but a perpetual scowl.

Audra reached into Rina's rolling case and found a binder decorated with symbols and cats dressed up as druids, wizards, and rogues. "Rin keeps pre-made characters on hand for newbies. Did you two think of a class for...?"

"Mandy."

I almost didn't recognize Mandy's voice when I thought I'd heard them all. The 'work' voice, the 'Shut the hell up, Caleb' voice, though mostly I was privy to Mandy's normal 'friend voice.'

But now this... sounded like a new voice. And I couldn't quite place this Mandy's voice.

Oh, God. Now I had to act cool in a *completely different way?*

Double shit! What had we talked about for a class for Mandy? Because we had talked about this...

"Well," Arcane stole the seat next to me, and an 'eep' escaped. "Loverboy is a bard..."

"Yes, they're all mind readers," Rina answered before I could bother asking.

How did these people get these powers, and - more importantly - how could *I* get the same powers?

Continuing as if I had done nothing so geeky as squealing again, Arcane said, "We got a bard, Rin's druid..."

I sucked in a loud gasp that made the room turn. "Stop! You're a druid?"

"Not her first character. But she's damn good at keeping her characters alive until they're too high level, and we force her to start over because she'd one hit kill a freaking boss." Arcane beamed.

Motherly warmth spread over Audra when she added, "Our little Rin-rin! Can't talk to anyone, a badass at the dragon."

"Cleric," Rina responded. "They're a ranger and rogue. Cisco's a bard. She'll balance us out. Even if Audra joins."

Audra

Why was it Rina mentioning *me* playing made my face turn itchy? "No! I'm... good." Before I could start stuttering like Rina, I flipped through the book. The girl legit had too much time and talent on her hands sometimes. She made characters solely to create characters. And in the case of Rin's characters, she usually makes sketches for each.

Also, she hates it when people move slowly. So, to calm the danged girl down, I had to flip leisurely through the book until...

"You passed the clerics," Rina snapped. "Alphabetical order."

"I did?" I said as if she didn't have everything in alphabetical order since she'd learned the alphabet back in kindergarten.

Rina incredibly carefully got down, as if she'd only realized now how high up she stood, and came to flip through the book. "Elbywynn would be good. Half-elf. Has some good starter spells." Pulling out the character sketch, Rina fully took over. She hefted the binder from me to also remove the character sheets.

"You, uh," I motioned at the corner of Cisco's mouth. "Drool."

"Ok! Well," Arcane clapped his hands and boomed in his most theatrical voice, "Shall we begin?"

Extricating myself from the chair, I found the comic I was reading and stationed myself behind the counter again. Except I wasn't really reading. My eyes kept straying to Mandy as Arcane introduced their tale.

Mandy

I have gotten used to feeling like the third, fifth, or seventh wheel. Rina, however, was entirely too sweet to let that happen. But she also kept up her shy streak, which surprisingly kept Cisco in a dopey loop, but it was cute, not annoying. As soon as the game started, Cisco returned to his usual self.

"I cast Hideous Laughter," Cisco pointed at Arcane with a flourish as if he held a magic wand.

"Again?" the guys at the end of the table whined.

"Come on! If it works, they're incapacitated. Makes it that much easier to kill the orcs!"

"It's dumb." The Arcane-like clone complained. "You have stronger spells! Use one of those."

But Arcane was already rolling his dice and then started laughing uncontrollably.

"See," Cisco relished in Arcane's over-the-top acting.

It was adorable. And I guess this hadn't been a waste of an afternoon.

"Yeah, well, next up in the order is Elby-wimp, and she has nothing to hit the orc with!"

"We should have re-rolled the order. A bard first is so stupid..."

"No, re-rolling!" Arcane hummed.

"And you're wrong," Audra sang as well. It was funny how similar Arcane and Audra were, like brother and sister.

I had no idea what Audra was getting at. Goodness, she was pretty, too. Looking at her made me squirm. She was cool, flipping through another comic, barely looking up. Sometimes, she seemed psychic about what would happen next.

"Come *on*," our *lovely* (note the extreme sarcasm) ranger ground out.

Right. It was my turn. "Uh..." I looked over the sheet again, which was super confusing. There were spells and moves, but the labeling and...

"You don't have Sacred Flame, but you have Toll the Dead," Audra appeared behind me, whispering. But not so close that I could feel her talking in my ear. Pity...

"I cast... Toll... the... dead?" I said.

As he made a show of it, Arcane rolled, but then, as he tossed the dice into his tray, he pantomimed being hit. "Aaaaaargh...." He tossed another die, this time an eight-sided die, straight at me. "Roll... for... damage... for me..."

The dice fell out of my hand in the most unemphatic roll of the night. "Uh... four?"

"Like that's going to do anything to an orc?" One of the guys—I seriously couldn't tell anyone their names if I had tried seeing as they were not worth learning— said. "Ugh... Lightning arrow at orc number 1."

Cisco stood so fast he knocked over his chair. "Whoa! Elbywynn is in range. Want to rethink that?"

"Nope." The clone of Arcane shook his head.

And no matter how attractive he might have been, the dude grinned viciously at me.

"Ok, my man, that's not cool," Arcane pushed the map forward. "You've got enough abilities…"

"Lightning." He locked eyes with me. "Arrow. Roll a dexterity saving throw if you're in range."

Rina was… well, characteristically quiet. Hunched, she kept sketching against her knees while she played. I didn't think she could even see the top of the table, but she rolled and said, "19." And placed a card up on the table, face down. Apparently, I could do math but not tell whether… She rolled again, this time two die. "Half four is two damage."

Arcane's rolls netted some damage to both orcs, but not much more than my attack.

I looked over my character sheet again. "Uhhh…"

Still standing over me, Audra shook her head. "Dude, this isn't cool."

"Roll, baby cleric. Let's go." And there, in the most asshole move yet, he leaned across the folding table to clap in my face.

"Four," I sighed.

"Seriously? Two D8s could knock her out…" Cisco tried again, still on his feet.

"Rin?" Audra asked, but Rina tapped the face-down card and didn't reply.

I rolled again, two dice as well, and… "Fifteen. That's…"

"My turn." Rina's interruption startled me.

I felt a shift but couldn't tell what it was because I was blinded by the asshole beaming at me.

"Using Wild Shape," Rina turned over the card she'd placed in front of her. "And turn into a brown bear and rush forward ten feet to Orc #2." She slid the card across the map to the orc in question.

Continuing to mumble as she sketched a new drawing, Rina said, "I use multi-attack, hitting Orc #2 with my bite and..."

"Hey! Wait..." The asshole's face turned sheet white.

The other guy, our supposed paladin, grumbled, "It's only a five-foot attack radius. You're..."

Rina could not be stopped if anyone tried. "I use my claws and accidentally hit..."

"This is bullshit!"

As she passed Arcane, Audra picked up a bag of dice before swinging herself over the end of the table and knocking some of their papers to the floor. "Hearing the roar of Fiona," Audra nodded at Rina, who still had not looked up from her sketch. "Amira Stormaxe bursts through the cave entrance and shouts, 'Is that my bestie in trouble?'"

"Ooooooooh!" Arcane squeals. "It's about to go dooooooooown!"

Out of everything that had happened, this was the only time Rina looked up from her drawings. "Are you the DM or not?"

"Oh... right." A timid grin did not suit Arcane, yet there he was sheepishly grinning at Rina (of all people!). "You didn't roll for..."

"She doesn't need to roll yet." Audra's voice became husky. "She needs to answer her bestie."

"I mean... I had it handled, but..." And then Rina settled two sketches on the table. One of Elbywynn, which I could recognize since there was a basic sketch she made on the character sheet she gave me, and one of Cisco's bard, Rok Noteleaf.

Distracted by the card, Cisco took his character and plopped back in his chair. "Awww," he gushed and turned the card so I could see. "Rina, you captured my essence."

"Your essence is ridiculousness with a bit of nobleness." I tried not to sound disappointed. And obviously failed miserably. But the sketch of my now-dead character was cute.

A slap reverberated in the shop, so crisp I thought Audra slapped one of the guys, not the table.

Somehow, Rina continued her distracted mumble, "With the +4, I got 24; his armor class is..."

"God, this set was overrated! Come on."

"Well," Arcane stood, straightening his scarf around his neck. "We don't take too kindly to people being ruder than a hidden recluse of a dwarf." He moseyed around the cash register, picking something up as he went around to the other side of the table, flanking the two guys. "You're not welcome back in my game or—" *Snap.* "—my store."

Chapter Twenty

The long way around

Mandy

The entire rest of the game was a blur in the best way possible. Audra never stopped her witty commentary, and without the other guys, Rina finally loosened up and stopped hiding behind her sketchbook.

Butterflies exited my stomach and flew into my lungs and brain whenever Audra glanced at me. Arcane fell back in his chair and announced, "The Orc King is defeated," but I didn't see or hear him. "Slain on his throne, our brave adventurers come forward..."

Rina narrowed her eyes, as did Audra. Both kicked out under the table, and Arcane jumped. "Ah!" Which got my attention.

"We roll..." Audra started.

"...perception," Rina finished, rolling her sparkling pink and purple glitter-infused die. "Oh, nat 20, huh?"

"If you weren't so good to have around for newbies," Arcane grumbled. "There are no traps. The Orc King was not nearly intelligent enough to set anything else. You find a boon hidden under the throne and..."

My stomach gurgled, cutting off the treasure description.

"Oh," Cisco twisted around, searching for a clock. "It's been four hours?"

Arcane checked his watch. "Well, I think you all took a longer way around..."

Audra threw a wadded-up scrap of paper she'd been doodling swirls on and doing math for her character sheet. "*I* did what I did to keep Elbywynn alive. Your stupid forest would have killed her instantly, you dork!"

"Let's," Arcane stood quickly, almost knocking the table over, "get some dinner." And then squealed like Cisco—who also squeaked again hearing his literal idol squeal, and it was a squealfest I could have done without hearing ever again. Arcane added, "And drinks! Oh, come on... I'll call Brandon, and we can all go out!"

"Breathe," I whispered to Cisco, concerned he'd pass out.

Behind me, a presence made the butterflies come to life again. "Seriously, dude. My cousin isn't *that* exciting." *Audra exuded a cool calm laced with a hint of annoyance.*

"Lover boy has taste! He's excited to hang out more!" Arcane exclaimed as if there may be a ringing ovation. "Obviously!"

Audra hung near my shoulder, her eyes drinking in every ounce of me—unless it was my wild imagination that usually was as wild as plain, unseasoned rice.

"Rina, your boy might need his head checked if he's so excited to hang out with that guy!" Leaning closer to my shoulder, I felt every inch of me stiffen. "Rin? Come on! You can't just sketch through drinks!" Audra laid a lazy arm around my shoulder—God, her musky perfume enveloped me. A scent so familiar, yet I couldn't place it. The scent was comforting and mellow. "Does she do that stuff at work? It's like a mystery how she operates when she's someplace I can't be."

That required me to actually think and my brain to function, which it wasn't.

"I do work in meetings. Not sketching," Rina said, nonplussed and not looking away from her sketch of another of our characters.

Cisco threw all her papers together, including my character sheets, and I felt the knot Rina became. All the papers were out of order. She'd spend however long putting every paper back in its place. I almost pulled myself out of Audra's grip, but it was weird... watching Cisco backtrack. He realized what he'd done and plopped back down with Rina to sort. Sitting with her, Cisco's furious blush accompanied some cute gestures, like touching her elbow to gently grab her attention...

"They are literally the cutest," Audra heaved a sigh, her arm squeezing my shoulders.

I hugged my arms into my stomach, playing back how Cisco and Rina acted at work. "He's always been. Took Cisco long enough to find someone as kind as he is."

"So..." Audra's tone shifted. "There's nothing for me to worry about? No skeletons in Cisco's closet to unearth?" Her grip on my shoulders tightened further, drawing me into Audra and enveloping me in her scent. All the space in my chest filled with butterflies.

"Nope," the word came out strangled.

"Come on, party people!" Arcane threw a scarf around his neck, letting it wrap dramatically. "Brandon's getting us a reservation! He'll meet us at..."

"Realm of Rhyme?" Rina and Audra said in unison.

"I sense a theme," I laughed, and Audra's arm gave my shoulders one last squeeze before unfortunately releasing me.

"NO WAY! We've never been there! The waitlist is *insane*." Cisco returned to his base 'meeting Arcane is the best day of my life' squeakiness and cleared his throat. Then Cisco tried to bring his voice lower again. "We can... get... in?"

Audra

"It's no big deal. Brandon is part owner, and he gets us reservations. My cousin acts like it's such a flex." My grin traveled around the room, landing last on Mandy's gorgeous eyes again.

Damn. Like seriously, damn. Why are all the beautiful women like Mandy not into girls like me? What rotten, unlucky moon had I been born under? I'd spent most of the afternoon watching her, trying to get a sense of what or who Mandy liked. Clearly, it wasn't Cisco, or my dear Rin wouldn't have had a chance. I love my girl, but Mandy had her hands down beat in the drop-dead gorgeous meter.

We are talking, Mandy made my head go utterly fuzzy. If I had brains like Rin and knew there were women like Mandy around, I would have forced myself into computer-whatever-the-hell-Rin-does, whether or not I liked it.

Sigh.

At least we were heading to Realm of Rhyme. If my usual luck with ladies held out, Mandy wouldn't look twice at me, anyway. There'd be enough alcohol to forget Mandy and I were fifth and sixth wheels to the cutest couple of all time (Rin and Cisco) and the smoochiest couple of all time (my cousin and his beau).

Sure. With enough alcohol, I could forget Mandy was so pretty, so sweet, so curvy... so...

Rina

"Rina?" Cisco waved a hand in front of my face. "Rina?"

No way. Audra always kept her crushes super stuffed down. But she'd been hanging off Mandy in the most literal sense. *And* she couldn't keep her eyes off Mandy. For as much apple saucing pancakes as she gave me throughout life for being unable to speak my mind or tell someone I like them, she fruit tarte-ing couldn't do the same.

True, she'd had some real rough breakups. The last woman she dated was... a special... muffin, for sure.

I felt a pinch on my scalp. Cisco held a small lock of my hair and pulled again. "Sorry. I slipped." He nudged me playfully. "Where did you go?"

"Nowhere..." I heard the crack in my voice as I lied through my streudeling teeth. Audra heard it, too. Heck, Arcane threw a wicked grin my way. But I couldn't say it. I had to be sure otherwise, I might jinx the whole thing. If I believed in jinxes. Which I didn't. But I knew Audra did, and since she was the one making 'lovey eyes' at Mandy, I knew I was in for a world of 'Don't jinx it' the second I asked her for any clarification.

"Who's ready to kill some songs?" Arcane shimmied, making his scarf fall. He threw it back over his shoulder while adjusting his glasses.

"Are you paying for drinks?" Audra asked, tongue actually in her cheek.

He slid down his thick glasses and waggled his eyebrows at every-one. "Yes. But only because..."

"Nope!" I squeaked. "Don't say it!"

Pretending he had an earpiece in, Arcane belted out, "Rina's got a boyfriend!"

"Dude," Audra cried, "she's *had* a boyfriend for a while."

"I had not met him." A sickly green tinge came over Cisco's face even before Arcane shook him violently. "Seeing is believing. Let's go!"

Chapter Twenty-One
Realm of... schemes

Mandy

Rina—shy until she will rip Caleb's balls off in a meeting Rina—can sing. It seemed Cisco had no access to this information. No, wait. Completely blindsided would be the best term.

But there she was, three drinks in—another sight I seriously never expected to see—on stage with Audra. They belted some unfamiliar Broadway song to a packed house in the Realm of Rhyme (generally like most other karaoke bars I'd been in crossed with a haunted house or dungeon aesthetic). Official analysis: Rina equals a conundrum.

"You alright there, slugger?" I tapped Cisco's shoulder with a playful punch, trying to knock a little life back into him.

He seemed to have not passed the awkward, gaping mouth and stunned silence phase of his shock. "I... Rina..."

Unlike Cisco, the shock remained short-lived, pretty much only until the next round of drinks came out.

"You can get it out," I said and sat back, twirling the end of the frozen cocktail around in the glass. Bright blue and named after something ridiculously simple sounding, like Mr. Cold or Mr. Frozen or something. The entire place was a geek haven for those who wanted to party like it was... a convention or something. But they certainly made a damn good drink.

"Wha..." Cisco glitched and seemed to gather his thoughts, but they spun around, unable to be caught.

I tried helping with, "Your Rina is like..."

"Oh," Arcane split the crowd on his return, a fresh pitcher of forget-the-night juice, his beau in tow with fresh glasses for the drinks. "Rina's a whole Banner situation when she drinks."

I dropped the stirrer in my drink, unsure how much more alcohol I could safely consume before mistakes were made. Embarrassing mistakes.

"Been like that for forever," Brandon held a sweet quality. I'd seen the guy around at bars before. Very VIP looks with high-end suits, but here he was dressed like Arcane in a fitted t-shirt and jeans (though far less tight). His brown waves fell gracefully and accented his chiseled jaw. But nothing about Brendan screamed geek. "Since we conned her into trying out for the musical sophomore year in high school!"

My turn to glitch. "NO!" I scanned the crowded tables around the roped-off VIP area close to the stage, then backed up at Audra and Rina. "Rina—that girl right there—was in theater?"

A flash caught Cisco and me off guard, and a guard (honest to goodness, black-suited guard) opened the rope and let another man in. He looked suspiciously like Rina. "Priceless," he chimed, then cackled. "She skewers another one. No one ever suspects Rina Takata to be... well, who she is, I guess." The guy flashed a suave smile at me. "Haru," and he extended his hand towards me. "Can't believe you stuck around," Haru grinned, leaning across the table, drawing Cisco's mouth closed with one finger. "This... is a lot to process. I get it."

Narrowing his eyes, I saw the calculations being made as Haru asked, "What if I told you she was Maria?"

We waited for more. Multiple musical lead characters have the name Maria. This was...

"Come on! Does that mean nothing?" Haru whined, and I could feel the same desperation as when Rina complained at Caleb in a meeting. No doubt about those two being related.

Rina

The monitor with the lyrics wavered. Ooooh... I'd most assuredly had too much to drink. If I remembered when I got sober again, I would give Brendan an applesaucing hard time. He probably made the drinks stronger on purpose. I'd only had... one... three... two? Wait...

Audra snatched my shoulders and shook hard amid jumping up and down...and up... and....ooof.

"AAAAAAH! We need to get our butts here more often! Oooh, the rush!" Audra screeched. Thank goodness we'd finished the song.

The applause and screams made my head swim more. A firm yank pulled me to the side stairs for the stage and down two before stopping, and my vision blurred, then focused for a moment before I saw Audra primping her hair. "How do I look?"

On the stairs, the stage lights weren't as blinding. I may have been wibbly wobbly, but I could see our table. And Mandy. I reached out, missed Audra's hair, tried again, and smoothed her hair behind her ear. I must have gotten some because she smiled at me.

I stumbled over nothing, and Audra caught me. "Come on, girlie."

I wanted to get something out (that was preferably not alcohol, instead of anxiety, induced vomit), but Audra dragged me through a sea of people pushing and colors, and before my brain caught up again, Haru was in my face with his phone, and Audra plastered her cheek to mine.

But once the flash had finished blinding me all over again (I'd really forgotten how bad stage lights were) and Cisco had my arm and a chair, all I could see was Audra and her eyes glued to Mandy. In that sweet, falling love sort of way. Dumplings, I needed to do something! Anything! Audra already seemed to have given up before she started!

And another glass, bright neon blue, waved in front of my face. I pushed it away before that threat of vomit became a reality.

Mandy bit her lip and shook her head... maybe at me... perhaps at Audra... possibly us both. I choked and grabbed Cisco, dragging him up. Mandy and Audra stood, both concerned and reaching for me. I stumbled again, this time landing on my knees before anyone could catch me. Mandy's purse was on the floor. I shoved my hand inside. *It had to work.*

Someone with a tender grip helped me up. Cisco. Of course, it was Cisco, and his sweet worry etched everywhere on his face. I pushed him back towards the ropes. With his usual suspicion, Haru watched us in a way only a brother could make his sister's skin crawl.

"Where are we going?" Cisco stopped me, and though he brought his lips up to my ear, I could barely hear him when he yelled again, "Where are we going?"

Away from alcohol. That was the first place. Because any more of Brandon's drinks and I would be in danger of making more mistakes than I ever made in my life. Spoken mistakes and... I don't know, physical?

"I need to talk to you," I said, trying to scream, but my stomach was ready to betray me. Yet again.

Every door guard and bouncer knew me. One even tried to get me a coat, even though I didn't come in with one. Once outside, Cisco pushed my glasses up and brushed my cheek, and all thoughts bled away. Even ones focused on my stomach.

"Where's Mandy's car?" I started.

Preemptively, Cisco quickly jerked away to cover his ears.

"Sorry," I shouted for some reason. "Where's Mandy's car?"

Cisco didn't answer fast enough, so I mashed buttons and heard the car beep around the back.

"Rina?" He called after me. "Rina! What's going on?"

Taking my wibbles and wobbles around the side of the building, Cisco called after me again. When he caught up, out of breath, he turned me around. "You are fast. And full of surprises today. I'm... I need to breathe..."

"Does Mandy like Audra?" I blurted out.

"What?"

Had he not heard me? Was I shouting loud enough or too loudly? "I mean... like... girls... well, women. Because it would be weird if she didn't like girls..."

"Oh," Cisco said and fanned himself. "Yeah, sometimes. Depends on the girl. I mean, woman." He sucked in huge, gasping breaths. "Why are you asking?"

I clicked the remote again. "I need you to do something to Mandy's car!"

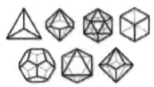

Cisco

I cleared my ears. "Repeat that, please." We both saw the lights flash on Mandy's car. God, I should have gotten those keys from Rina sooner. Drunkenly, she kept mashing buttons.

"Hey, is Rin ok?"

Oh, thank God! Backup.

Arcane came around the corner, and Rina made a silent gasp, then flapped her hands quickly. "Perfect!"

"That's not a look I want to see, Rina!" And with that, Arcane began backing away with his hands up.

"No, come on! Help me!" Another fast move by Rina, and she'd caught Arcane in her stumbling grip. "Audra is smitten over Mandy, and she's all frozen up, and all I need to do is get her into... into..."

Poor Rina ran out of steam, or the alcohol-induced fuzziness had become too strong.

Behind me, Arcane tapped my shoulder in a steadily quickening succession. "Drunk Rina's antics are not..."

"One bed!" Rina shouted, turning the heads of people waiting in line to get into Realm of Rhyme. "Or... you know those romance stories where the couple gets trapped together, and they have no choice but to... kiss and admit their feelings for each other!"

"Drunk Rin would try this and trap you in an elevator and potentially vomit on whoever is trapped with her," Arcane murmured to me. "I suggest you run. If you want to keep some semblance of your relationship intact."

Little did Arcane know how much of Rina's vomit I had stomached thus far. More than most would think. And I didn't even succumb once to my own retaliatory vomit, thank you very much!

Rina, or maybe a clone/imitation of Rina, hopped up and down. "Break her car, Cisco! Or at least something easily fixable but not fixable tonight. Audra can borrow Wes' car to take Mandy home, and boom!" Rina clapped, hands out like she'd presented the most brilliant idea.

"I don't think she's thought this through. Look," Arcane spun me around, making me dizzy. "We take Rina home..."

Arms wrapped around my neck and shoulders in an awkward hug, still bouncing. "Please??? Don't take this from your cousin," she jabbed Arcane, "and your best friend!" Then Rina stabbed me with her finger, too.

"Ugh," I sighed. "Rina, Arcane's probably right."

"I love my cousin," Arcane added. "That's why I'm nixing this whole stupid drunk Rina plan. Sorry."

"Pleeeeeeease?" she begged. "When was the last time Audra swooned over someone?"

"Stop," Arcane poked Rina's nose.

"I don't know about Audra," I offered, weirdly getting invested. "But for Mandy, it's been a hot minute."

Wrong thing to say.

Rina—calm, gentle, Rina - emitted such a loud squeal that it impaired my hearing in one ear for a while. "Oh, God. Ok, give me the keys." My ear rang while I opened Audra's car hood.

Standing off to the side, Arcane shook his head. "Rina?" He looped an arm around her shoulder, but more like he was about to throw her in a headlock. "I never should have let Brandon make the drinks. Stop the madness, please."

"Your cousin deserves love," Rina demanded, shaking his arm off her.

In the black of night, with only a few streetlights to illuminate the engine, I popped off one lead to the battery and shoved it down. Then I grabbed a spark plug and took it out as well. Older cars tended to be much easier to fiddle with. I could reach other wires, but Mandy's car was new enough that there was little to grab. The engine was tightly packed. "Good enough," I said and lowered the hood.

"I cannot believe I am saying this, but I'll get it towed…"

"Just tow it to my house. I'll fix it in the morning." I turned right into Rina. Her cheeks were flushed pink, and her nose, too. It was weird; I'd never seen her with such a goofy grin. She threw herself at me and kissed me. In public.

"Oh my," Arcane squeaked, turned to leave, and squeaked again! "Mandy! Audra!"

"Is everything… oh. OH!" Mandy screeched, and while Rina continued to kiss me, I kind of thought I might have heard the others retreat. But Rina also melted my brain.

And I still couldn't hear out of my one ear.

Chapter Twenty-Two
Dude is not applicable

Rina

"You drank over the weekend," Caleb sidled beside me while I waited for the coffee to brew in the break room.

"For the love of blueberry pancakes, Caleb..." This is why I didn't enjoy drinking. And loathed Brandon's drinks. The headache lasted days, no matter how much I battled dehydration. Plus, I didn't do *any* *art* all weekend. Which amounted to a useless weekend.

Caleb smirked. "Some things never change, I guess. Did Audra take you somewhere?"

"We went out after Wes' game." My brain might have been trying to explode out from behind my eyeballs.

"Did Francisco see this?" Caleb's signature cockiness drenched his words, and I grimaced. "Oh, he did? And what did *you* do after said drinks?"

Instead of answering, I poured not nearly enough coffee into my Lazy Beans mug and turned as Mandy passed the breakroom. "Ah, buttermilk biscuits."

Audra had been MIA all weekend after karaoke. I texted and called but got nothing back. Maybe I should have texted more, but my post-inebriated state did not allow it. Jogging after Mandy, I tried to concentrate on not spilling my liquid savior (aka the coffee) and what I would ask. However, my mind became empty when I skidded past Mandy's door, backtracked, and saw Mandy sitting at her desk, about to log onto her computer. "Hey, Mandy," I tried, leaning against the door frame. But I had to try several angles, and could I look natural putting my hand on my hip? No, I was holding my coffee mug. What would I do? Rest my mug against my hip?

"Smooth," Caleb joined me in the door. Why the raspberry jam did he join me?

I still didn't know what to do with my hands, arms, or... any part of my body. Still, I persisted and asked, "So, get home, alright?"

She gave me a strange look and smirked at Caleb, who was more busy watching me than Mandy. "Fiiiiine."

"Yeah?" My blasted free hand still couldn't decide where it wanted to be. "Nothing... interesting happened?"

"Oh," Caleb sipped his coffee. "*That's* what you were up to."

Mandy glared at us both, similar to how my mom would stare into my soul when she thought I might be lying. "What is going on?"

"I... have got a call... I need to be on," I tried checking my watch but apparently forgot to wear one, so I looked very cool staring at my blank wrist. "I'll catch you at lunch."

For some inane reason, Caleb followed me to my office. Even standing watch over me while I called Audra and put her on speakerphone.

"What the pastry puff is wrong with you?" I melted into my chair and smooshed my face into my hands.

"Good morning to you, too, sunshine. Why the hell are you waking me up?"

"Rina was drunk this weekend, huh?" Caleb settled himself in my guest chair and picked up my notepad, scrawled with notes for the AI interface.

"Hi, asshole," Audra sighed, and I felt her renewed exhaustion. Yes, Caleb did have that effect everywhere he went, both on the phone and in person.

"Charming. And you expected *her* to ask out Mandy?" He flipped the page sharply, and both Audra and I groaned.

Audra snapped, "Kick him out, Rin."

But I felt a gurgle, and though it wouldn't do any wonders for my stomach, I gulped down my coffee. "Answer the question, Audra."

"Oh, Lord, I knew you were up to something!"

"Audra did not do what you wanted, Rina." Caleb pointed and tapped the desk hard, pointing at the pad when I glared at him through my fingers. "This is a good plan. Who needs to be put on this part of the project?"

A long pause drew out before Audra heaved a heavy sigh. "I got cold feet, ok. Happy?"

"No, not happy." For many reasons, I was not happy. Did I eat breakfast? Breakfast might have helped me be happier, less cranky, and less hung over.

"Dude..." Audra groaned.

"Rina's a girl. Dude is not applicable," Caleb interrupted her.

"I will smack the shit out of you," Audra snapped. "Mandy is super hot, and funny and smart and... I am not her type. I can tell. So, I didn't bother, and instead, we had a nice, completely awkward drive home."

"That's not true," I said, but trying to find more to add... I just couldn't. How familiar was I with Mandy? I hadn't been working with her for long. I should have asked Cisco more questions about Mandy. Gotten to know her a bit better.

Caleb tossed the notepad on the papers littering my desk and propped his feet on the scant inches of free space at the desk's corner. "You can't know if you two are an appropriate fit if you don't try."

I lifted my head. Did I hear Caleb right?

"Tell me you created an AI that sounds like Caleb. Because that *almost* sounded nice. And like..."

Giving us a curt shrug, Caleb sipped his coffee. "I want Rina to actually get to work. Otherwise, she might start plotting your next date while sober. And no good ever comes of that. So, are we all agreed? Audra will grow some metaphorical balls and ask Mandy out?"

"I really want to hate you still," Mandy said; sleep finally faded from her voice.

My phone buzzed with a new text. The flag caught my eye. Audra's mom.

I gaped as I read the text. "Ah! Your dad's promotion! The dinner to celebrate!"

Audra drawled with the impending torture, "...is Friday. I know."

"Ask Mandy! Go to the dinner and have an excuse to cut out early!" Because, back to the whole Mandy's Aunt Chelsea is a big fat... cinnamon... no, that's an insult to cinnamon rolls. Hmmm....

Audra perked up. "What are you going to do? Cover for me?"

"I'll bring Cisco. Your mom never thought I'd date someone again after *a certain... break up*." Caleb didn't seem put off by my glare. "And Wes will be there. It'll be fine."

"How did you get invited to Audra's father's promotion dinner?" Caleb asked, staring forlornly into his now empty coffee mug. Anyone would have thought the coffee grounds were more interesting to Caleb than the conversation.

I'm pretty sure Audra stared at her phone as I stared at Caleb now. Incredulously. "Because we've been best friends for so long, we're like sisters. It happens when you have close friends." As genius as Caleb was, he should have been able to figure that out. He'd known Audra almost as long as he'd known me.

Caleb rolled his eyes, then said, "That's annoying."

"You're annoying," I grumbled. At least it earned me a little applause from Audra.

Caleb tapped the papers and repeated, "We need to get someone on this part of your project ASAP."

Chin in my hand, I waited for Caleb to leave. Which he did promptly.

"Is he gone?" Audra asked.

"Yes."

"How do you work with that asshole?"

"Language," I said on reflex.

A hard edge came to Audra's tone. "You are literally surrounded by adults."

Banana bread. I couldn't do this any longer. "Ask Mandy to your dinner, or I will! It's not like it would be a big shock or anything. You've brought home girls before."

"I brought home a girl or two to just my parents. Aunt Chelsea remains convinced, to this day, that they were my friends when it came up at parties. My mom refuses to correct her, and no one says much to Wes and Brandon because of denial. Pretty sure everyone is in denial outside of mom, dad, and Wes." All fair points that I had clearly forgotten. Some friend I was. Or I could blame my post-inebriated state. "And it's not like a family dinner would be a good place for a first date."

"I met Cisco's entire family on our first date!"

"Remind me, how many times did you throw up that night?" At least Mandy finally sounded relaxed.

I was running out of pastries. Peach Cobbler! Chalk up another point to Audra. Why was her brain far more functional than mine?

I leaned close to the phone and whispered, "Your Aunt Chelsea is a..."

"Yes?" Audra asked skeptically.

"Pizza flipper!"

"I knew you wouldn't go through with a real swear. Don't worry, Rin. When I bring someone home... I'll give it to Chelsea. I just don't think it's in the cards for me and Mandy."

I doubted very much that Audra would say a single syllable to Chelsea. Audra's gone on for years about what she might do, but no one ever stood up to Chelsea or Audra's mom's older sisters. They were all like Chelsea.

Listening to Audra continue, a pang rang in my heart when she said, "And you realize everyone assumes you and I are going to get married."

It had come up before. When Audra and I lived together during college, there were many side eyes and whispered conversations. "I love you, but that's not happening," I said.

"It's not like," I heard Audra smiling, "I can take you away from Cisco. He's too sweet. Especially fixing Mandy's car like he did."

I froze. Banana pudding. I forgot about Mandy's car. "Yeah. He's a gem." Before she could ask anything else, I rushed to add, "Gotta get to work. Talk to you later. Ask Mandy about Friday; maybe you can get out of the dinner altogether! Ok, bye!" And hung up.

Smooth, Rina. Real blueberry streudal-ing smooth.

Mandy

Oh. Shit. Well, I certainly felt like an idiot. I was utterly blind. And where the hell did all these sides of Rina come from? The girl had more devious bones in her body than Caleb. No wonder... ooooh! I can't believe it. Her brother had been right. No one expected this side of Rina. Ever.

Chapter Twenty-Three

New information. Caleb isn't a robot AND has feelings

Mandy

Back-to-back meetings had me running around in circles and on client calls so constantly that by the time I was free to stop by Cisco's office, he'd left for the day.

I never got Audra's phone number, so I couldn't just text and ask her out. Why was I so stupid? She was a barbarian with a shining axe... well, truth be told, Rina had saved my character first. Whatever! It didn't matter. What mattered was how stupid I'd been. Had I really not noticed her flirting? Was I dense or overly cynical? My stomach felt like it was tied in knots and filled with flutters.

All of which I ignored. And why?

"Because nothing ever goes right," I mumbled as I scrolled through my work emails. More than a dozen new emails came in within the last hour, not to mention my backlog.

"Are you talking about work?"

"Caleb!" My knee banged into the bottom of my desk, snagging my tights on a sharp edge and leaving a gash that stung like a bitch.

"Or are you talking about Audra?" He checked his watch and then glanced at me icily. "Wasn't there a report due today?"

If Caleb had more to say, he didn't add it and instead moved down the hallway.

"Don't you ever go home?" I called after him.

Caleb's echoed call came back from the hallway, "Don't you ever open your eyes? Not the first person you missed flirting with you!"

I processed that for a hot minute. "Who the fuck flirted with me?" Forgetting the pain, I raced after Caleb — not an action I ever thought any woman in their right mind would ever have — and let out a piercing whistle. That got his attention. "Who?" I demanded.

Caleb turned with the same bored expression he gave everyone. "Francisco somehow figured it out first."

"Cisco flirts with everyone." Oh, I'd run for no reason. Ow! "That doesn't count. He stopped..."

"He figured out that you had no interest in any of the guys here. I'm still not sure how he did that." The hallways were dead silent. Caleb leaned into the wall, arms folded. "And I'm exhausted by trying to weasel work into navigating all my employees' interpersonal relationships—relationships that should stay outside of work."

Oh, no! Caleb would not get a dig in like that. "Says the guy who insisted on hiring his ex-girlfriend."

Caleb fixed his chilling eyes on me again. "She's the best..."

No one could argue with that.

Everything crashed: my brain, my energy, and my will to do literally anything, including moving from this very spot.

"You haven't dated in a while," Caleb mumbled.

"Neither have you!" The retort had little oomph behind it.

"Mandy," And my heart—my wretched, stupid heart—actually felt Caleb had a single ounce of sincerity. What the hell was going on? "You go out to forget things. And never anywhere you can meet someone of substance. So what's the reason behind that?"

"Excuse me?" My heart skipped a beat, but then it tried to race to catch up again. "I refuse to date someone I work with."

An almost—*almost*—human shrug from Caleb made him appear so normal. "That's something to tell yourself."

Caleb's stupid shrug and stupid nonchalance made me want to squeeze his stupid head! How had he gone from sincere to ass in a single breath?

I muttered, "What the hell do you know about me? Huh?"

"I know that when you first started here at Infinite, you were in a relationship." Lazy, stupid, Caleb pulled out his phone, burying himself in it. I expected him to leave, but then he asked, "Do I need to pry? Because this is tiresome."

"That has nothing to do with—"

But Caleb interrupted me. "Does it have anything to do with you avoiding someone who could be with you for more than one night?"

What? *What?*

"What about you? You're so keen to dive into my personal life, but you tried asking Rina out again." He wants to keep personal stuff out of work, but he doesn't keep his personal feelings out, either!

"Admittedly, Rina and I were... well suited to each other. Or so I thought." His eyes found mine, and there, deeply embedded where no one could see Caleb's feelings, there lived hurt. "I made a mistake." He didn't say it cost him, but I knew.

"You?" My voice went up an octave. Impossible! "A mistake?"

There's always a first time for everything. Including Caleb admitting he made a mistake.

"It might be for the best. She chose to date Cisco, a concept I will never understand." He pocketed his phone and gave me his un-nervingly undivided attention. "I answered your questions. Now you answer mine."

Down the hall was Cisco's office. Bright-colored lights swirled out into the hallway. Probably a light machine he'd left on if he wasn't asleep in his office. "I worry about Cisco and Rina. Working together and falling in love... maybe not with you around."

A hint of a smile crept onto Caleb's face. "I'll take that as a com-pliment."

"It wasn't one." Staring down at my leg, I got a better look at the cut and my tights. Maybe if I ignored the question long enough, Caleb would take the freaking hint.

"It was never a phase," Caleb said. "And that's just a fact. However, that's not what bothers you about Audra."

"What?"

Still somehow sounding bored and studying his impeccably clean nails, Caleb continued, "Your mom. I remember a conversation I overheard. But I'm starting to think..."

"You really collect all the freaking tea in this place but have no one to tell it to, huh?" How the *hell* had he heard that? *When* the hell had he heard that?

"You'd be surprised. Rina taught me a lot. Anyway, it's not a phase." God! Those eyes of Caleb's sent a shiver down my spine. I couldn't tell if it was because he actually had feelings to share or that maybe, somewhere deep inside, he actually understood... me. He added in the most unhelpful manner, "And continuing to go out and sleep around won't get you a relationship—not unless you try. Take a leap or whatever the saying is."

"That's..." I stopped. He wasn't wrong.

"There are worse people to consider dating than Audra Taylor." The silence hung between us until he said, "Namely, dating Francisco Reyes."

Taylor? I had no idea what her last name was.

Caleb sighed. "I'm going home. I don't have her number. Ask Rina. And do something quickly before Rina continues her insane plotting."

Plotting? Yeah, I hadn't gotten a chance to call Cisco out on... wait. Rina was the one plotting, but... Francisco Reyes... you little shit!

He was in on it, too!

I returned home to darkness, as I did every night. The door clicked closed, echoing in the cavernous living room. Most of my apartment was bare. I had a couch and a dining table that could not quite fit two people. Caleb's annoyingly poignant words picked at the broken pieces of my life. Tears pushed against my eyes, threatening to spill at any moment. I never answered Caleb's questions.

Slapping the light on, my heels clicked across the wood floor until I flicked them off and left them haphazardly in the middle of the living room for easy tripping access when I woke in the morning. I'd forgotten all about the gash in my leg until I took off my torn tights. And left them in the middle of the floor too, but they were less of a worry or tripping hazard.

I just wanted to clean the wound and rest, not relive the day and hear Caleb's annoying remarks. Opening the medicine cabinet, though, was like a proverbial slap to the cheek.

"How am I supposed to compete?" Mia yelled.

The only person I'd ever lived with. The only person I really ever loved before.

"Convenient how you found a job with all those hot guys."

"Why would that matter?" We'd attended the open house at *Infinite Labs, which was primarily for elementary children and their parents but open to the public. Loads of families came through, but Caleb and Dr. Wellington insisted that since I was new, I should just attend and learn more about all the lab departments and get to know my new coworkers.*

Mia hadn't stopped huffing since meeting Caleb in the only place he'd ever seemed charming... ever. Somehow, there was a magical or hidden switch on that frigid man when families were around.

"Am I supposed to compete with them? You're the one that's got it bad for..."

"Where is this even coming from?" I always asked Mia the same *question when she'd rant like this.* "We've been together for years!"

I closed the cabinet, shocked at the person staring back. Pale, possibly even ashy. Sweaty with deep bags under her eyes, staring back at me. After cleaning off the wound and changing into pajamas, I stared at my bed. It had been my bed for well over a decade.

It was one of the few places Mia and I shared she didn't take. Every night for several years now, alone in the dead of night, when I tried to get the courage to slide into bed, it felt foreign and wrong.

"What did you do to our bed?" Mia snapped.

All I'd done was get new sheets—the super-soft Egyptian Cotton—a splurge since I'd gotten my first paycheck. I could get something ex-tra—something special but that I would use every day. Ugh, after I'd put them on, I'd rolled around and snuggled with the pillow. I could have fallen asleep right there.

"Do you know how much that costs?" Mia'd continued, "It was a waste of money! Or is that all you can do now? Throw your money in my face?"

"I didn't..."

My stomach churned again as I backed out of the bedroom. Drunk or drunk and with a stranger for the night, that bed, those sheets, were easier to take with the memories bombarding me. I could forget them in the haze of alcohol. My anti-social outings, as I called them. I didn't go out to be social. But to forget.

Right now? Sober and alone... I shut the door and fell onto the couch. It wasn't just my mom's comments that haunted me. How the hell did Caleb see right through me?

Chapter Twenty-Four
Bubble gum pink

Mandy

I had zero sleep, tossing and turning all night as I fumed. It wasn't a good look, I know, but here I sat in Cisco's office chair, already on my second cup of coffee, watching his light show sparkle across the various machines in varying states of completion. I sat and watched... and waited.

"Holy shit!" Cisco popped around the door, jumped out of his skin (the least he could do after trying to set me up), and dropped everything he carried. His stainless steel coffee mug rang on the floor while papers flew all around, floating down like huge snowflakes. "Mandy! What are you doing here?"

"Did you set me up?" I didn't think I'd be mad enough to scream. Alright, I wasn't screaming, but I was close to it.

"That... was not my plan." Instead of picking up his mug, Cisco backed out of the door. "Rina, she was drunk and..."

I advanced. "Did you break my car on purpose?"

"I... *fixed* your car." Cisco's voice cracked, and he tried to swallow a lump in his throat.

Still, I kept advancing on Cisco.

"Ask out Audra!" he screeched, perched on one leg and curling into a ball against the hallway wall.

I prided myself on not hitting him. "How? How am I supposed to do that?"

"Uh..." Cisco unfurled one arm enough to dig into his pocket and take out his phone. "I have her number. Rina gave it to me."

It was right there... within reach. A simple path to less heartache. Or all the heartache. Pushing away, I caught myself in Cisco's office door. "I'm not...look, I'm not... in a place to ask anyone out." *Thump-thump-thump.* My heart vibrated, almost like I'd had too much coffee, but two cups wasn't my max. I fanned my hands and shook them out, pleading with whatever deity was out there to make this torture end. "Just please stay out of my love life. When I want to date someone, I'll date them."

There was no turning back. My heart hammered into my ribs wildly. I ran back to my office, hands trembling as I sank against my door to close it and slid down into a ball.

Rina

"You need a new car, dear." Audra's mom sat on Audra's other side. We crowded around her, and another chair, between me and Audra's mom, held foil strips, more latex gloves, and a bowl of mixed hair bleach.

My chocolate-chipping face grew red hot. I used a comb to divide a new section instead of answering Mrs. Taylor. Why were we still talking about me?

Audra's smirk crinkled her nose. "Cisco will fix it. Am I right?"

Of course, my car *broke down again!* It was a constant point of contention, but... how could I part with my baby? We had history, memories... mostly of me broken down places.

Mrs. Taylor leaned past Audra's back so fast that she yanked the strip of hair she held. But Mrs. Taylor shushed Audra and fixed me with a squinty glare. "Who is Cisco?"

"Her *boyfriend*," Audra sang.

I shrank back and tried to block out all sound while I painted the new strip of hair with bleach. "Traitor," I muttered. I'd tried to keep the news quiet. There'd be enough torture at the dinner.

"Oh, that's wonderful!" With bleach-covered gloves still on and even holding the brush full of bleach, Mrs. Taylor hopped up and came around for an attempt at a hug that didn't end with bleach spots on my t-shirt. "I knew you were glowing. And now you two need to tell me all about Cisco. Was that his name?"

Audra beamed. "He's pretty cool, mom. Wouldn't let him date our little Rin-rin if he weren't."

I tried to concentrate on folding the last foil I had finished and placing a new one, but I got an elbow to the knees, so I muttered, "He works with me at Infinite Labs."

"Your new job! That's right! How is working at Infinite? I always disliked that Virtek place. They were so rude. Your mother always said the same. She's very proud of you, love. All your family is." Mrs. Taylor's sweet rambling almost settled my pooling anxiety. Almost.

Sure. They just don't say it. It's different from how mom or dad were raised, so it doesn't seem necessary for them to say it.

"He's great. Cisco and his friend came and played Wes' game over the weekend. Wes and Cisco hit it off." Audra's unending ability to talk would keep going enough for both of us. Thank sugar cookies she had the superpower to talk to anyone about anything.

But Mrs. Taylor practically raised me. One glance around Audra again, and she saw *everything* with her unholy motherly sense. "There's more, isn't there?"

If I weren't already breaking out in hives, I would now. "Uh... no."

"He's a knight with a shining wrench." Dang, Audra! No, please don't tell your mother... "He fixed her car."

Audra's mom fanned herself with a gloved hand. "Man after my own heart."

"Well, one of you finally snagged a man." I froze mid-brush stroke on a new section of hair. Audra's Aunt Chelsea leaned against the counter. No one saw her come in. Like Audra's dad, she had brown hair that erred on the side of red but couldn't be called ginger, unlike Wes, who may have his picture in the dictionary under ginger. Aunt Chelsea's husband, Greg, was nice enough but never around. It wouldn't have changed her attitude if he were. Chelsea's snap comments rarely had a filter.

"Chels, chill," Audra's mom always tried.

But Aunt Chelsea waved her hand dismissively at us. "Not the one of you girls I thought would snag a guy. Rina has always screamed lonely cat lady."

Ugh.

"Chelsea!" Very few occasions made Audra's mom pull out her 'mom' voice.

I turned in on myself. It was impossible to make myself disappear *and* do Audra's hair, but a vice grip clamped onto my chest. Angry, venomous thoughts swirled—things I'd never say. *At least my cat is more congenial than you!* No, that wasn't enough. *I don't know how Greg...* Ah, second thought, that is too mean. How could I say something mean about Greg? Even in my head.

Chelsea snapped her fingers, thinking aloud, "Come on. Audra had that roommate..."

At that, Audra's jaw tensed, her teeth ground together, and I bumped into her chair with mine to get closer. "Ignore her," I whispered.

I knew she couldn't just ignore Aunt Chelsea. "Roommate, huh?" Audra gritted. "Like Wes and..."

"Oh, don't get me started on Wes. A lovely boy who has so much to offer. I don't understand him either."

"He's married..." Audra's mom started, and Chelsea cut her off.

"Yes, to his ridiculous shop." Chelsea snapped cabinet after cabinet open. "Who can make a living off comic books?"

"I want whatever Chelsea's on so I can be so freaking delusional," Audra said under her breath.

I folded another foil and smiled, but inside, another crack formed. *No one, especially Audra, deserved such crap in their lives.*

"Well, I hope Rina brings her beau to dinner tomorrow. Maybe Audra can take a page from Rina's book..."

"Chelsea," Audra's mom scolded, "Don't you have somewhere else to be?"

"Daniel asked me to make more coffee. We're taking a break from the sink repair." Giving a loud sniff, Chelsea watched as we continued to silently bleach strips of Audra's hair. "Maybe keeping to more natural colors would help, Audra."

My jaws ached with how hard I clamped down on my teeth. I almost wanted to actually bite my tongue since the pain might keep me from saying anything else. But Audra sighed, her gaze lingering on the bottles of hair dye, so I whispered, "Should have gotten a brighter bubble gum pink." And that got me a wan smile, which was better than nothing, I guess.

Chapter Twenty-Five

Pent up aggressions

Mandy

Cisco, possibly rightfully, avoided me. Sure, he claimed he wasn't actively trying to... but when he put Rina between me and him in the hallway as they walked back from lunch, I got the hint. I can't say I blamed him. The sneak attack was a little... over the top. Served him right, though. But even Rina flailed to get him off her and even batted him when he grabbed her shoulders—which was weird. I never would have imagined Rina lashing out at anyone, though now armed with the knowledge that she had a brother changed my views a bit. Siblings brought out strange behaviors in everyone. Including Rina. Of course, Rina... well, she's been nothing that I'd expected her to be.

And God damn it! Rina and Cisco were hard to stay mad at! They are all endearing and cute to one another. Like a perfect rom-com movie couple jumped off the screen into real life. I couldn't watch their overly sweet actions for long without my stomach cramping. Now, though, they were back at it. Cisco avoided me and Rina huffed about protecting him, but with little enthusiasm. All because Caleb—freaking *Caleb*—called a meeting. Supposedly on Dr. Wellington's behalf, but that remained to be seen.

To make matters worse, we had twenty freaking minutes before the end of the day. Twenty minutes of watching Cisco and Rina's tiny actions, quick smiles—or frowns—as Rina shot Cisco a glare when he stepped around Rina to put her between me and him again. He also sat in a chair across from me and turned toward Rina once we'd gotten to the boardroom. Angry cute facial expressions from Rina was still cute.

"I'll make this short and sweet," Dr. Wellington started quickly. *Thank goodness!* "I'll be heading to the AI Symposium hosted by AAAI in Vancouver. We're not presenting Rina and Caleb's work just yet, but the project looks promising for the next symposium, and I love the direction AAAI's conference is taking. While I'm away, though, Caleb will manage projects I was heading up."

Oh. Greeeeeeeeeat. The *most delightful news* to get any freaking given day—more time with Caleb freaking Williams.

The boardroom released a collective groan, for which Caleb rolled his eyes.

"Cisco, I want to review that order with you before the end of the day," Dr. Wellington shot Cisco a little mock finger gun. "I'm sorry if we're staying a little late. I want to get a few projects squared away. This was a last-minute change, and I'm heading out tonight..."

Jumping at his name, Cisco nodded enthusiastically, "Yes! Of course. I have a call scheduled with the manufacturers. Prices are going up because..."

Dr Wellington waved off the concern. "We'll eat the costs. Our current generation of CPUs and GPUs are...."

That's when the show really started. Holy crap, did it ever start.

Caleb huffed. "Based on the current capabilities, our farms' current GPUs and even CPUs are more than satisfactory for Rina's project."

"Nope," she snapped, tapping her pen on its end, spinning it around, and tapping the other end, each hit becoming more pronounced. "The crashing is..."

"Not related to the GPUs or the CPUs." And boy, Caleb really had the audacity to level a glare at Rina. Now that I knew her capabilities, that seemed dangerous. "It's the stability of the code."

"I fixed the code." With a heavy hand, Rina clicked the pen on the table. "Now it's the GPUs that cannot keep up."

"You're wrong," Caleb said without missing a beat.

"And you're an idiot," Rina said. The board room had fallen utterly silent. No one even dared to breathe, including me.

The last person who insulted Caleb, not even in front of Dr. Wellington, had their desk cleaned out for them before lunch. Granted, Rina's insult was disastrously pathetic, but it was an insult to Caleb's mental acuity, and he always took those seriously.

Before he could respond, Rina slammed her hand on the table—and on top of the pen, so she also winced—as she added, "I distinctly remember you undercounting bandwidth and memory capacity in our final project. Don't come at me with the same mistakes."

Cisco let out a squeak, startled by his phone's chirping alarm. "Ah, the call with N—"

"I'm not undercounting anything."

Where was popcorn when I needed it? Proverbial smoke billowed from Caleb. Dr. Wellington drummed his fingers on his legs, seemingly as invested as the rest of us were now.

Caleb snapped, "The GPU and even the CPU are not the issue. And it's shortsighted to keep wasting money on upgrades."

That's when Dr. Wellington came to kneel near Cisco. "I wish you'd brought snacks. What brought this on?"

See, popcorn. From now on, it was a necessary item at every meeting involving Caleb and Rina. I could quietly make that suggestion to Dr. Wellington. If anything, he'd give it a good laugh. I would have said something to Cisco, too, but seeing as I was still a bit peeved with him and he wouldn't talk to me, it would have to wait until he grew a pair.

"I do not know." Cisco silenced the alarm. Breaking away from the potential train wreck happening in front of him, Cisco sucked in a shuddering breath. "The call, sir?"

"Ugh," Dr. Wellington hummed. "I wanted to see how this played out. Fine. Mandy, walk with us; I need to get a final update on your work before I head out."

Damn it! I wanted to see how this played out too!

Rina

"Don't walk away," Caleb's sharp jabs were getting duller by the moment.

He could take his opinion and... stuff it in an uncrustable sandwich for all I cared! I. Was. Finished! Caleb Williams always knew best, huh? "I'll show you the damn GPU is the issue! I fixed..."

"Oh." He deflated. The board room where Dr. Wellington had called the meeting was eerily empty by the time I stomped out. Neither I nor Caleb heard Dr. Wellington dismiss the meeting. Odd. Caleb came around, arms crossed, and glared into my eyes. "These useless interpersonal problems need to be resolved. What happened now? Did Francisco screw up...?"

OOOOOOH! My breaths came shorter and quicker. "No!" And now my fists shook, nails digging into my hands as I tried to remember what Caleb's setup ran into his office. It was probably the same specs as my setup, possibly less since he wasn't testing the software... Scratch that. He absolutely tested everyone's projects without telling them. He would totally do that!

A fire burned in Caleb's eyes despite the strangely calm way he demanded, "Come to my office," Goodness, this was university all over again. "You were going to prove to me it was the hardware specs anyway..."

"Don't. Do. That!" I hated it when he read my mind! I hated Caleb! I hated technology! I hated... ARG!!!!! I followed Caleb to his pristine office, where he had perfectly organized every scrap of paper, notebook, and textbook on shelves and rolling carts. Circumventing him and the guest chair, I took Caleb's chair and logged in on his server with my credentials.

"Who pissed you off, Rina? Because, at this point, I want the Rina I prefer working with back. It's been three days of this."

After copying the latest file from my server to Caleb's, I ran it and waited after giving the AI a challenging prompt to execute. Fine... I could answer his stupid question. "Audra."

"You never fight with Audra. You're too nice."

"Thanks for that, I think." The fruit tarte-ing code spun and spun... I could practically see it huffing and puffing, just like I would do if I ever went out running. And from the corner of my eye... there Caleb was, just watching me so very calmly! "Fine! It wasn't Audra, but her aunt. And tonight, I have to go over there and not snap..." I slammed the enter key again. Something hung up in the program, and while

I knew deep down that hitting enter would do nothing to make the program move faster, I tried again. The equivalent of smashing the elevator button to make an elevator move faster! Wait. Why would I care if it didn't continue running? That was the point!

Across from me, sitting in his guest chair, Caleb remained utterly silent, so I felt obligated to add, "Are you not going to make any snarky comebacks?"

"I really just want your emotions to normalize so we can return to our typical working relationship."

"This is pretty fudge cake-ing typical," I grumbled. His computer whirred, the old fans kicking up to max to keep up cooling. *Finally! I brought up the hardware stats to watch the crash happen in real-time.*

"Would you even snap at Audra's aunt?"

Failure was imminent in the program and in my brain. "No! Of course not! That isn't useful. I just need to calm down and..." Oh, *come on!* The cooling evened out. The program continued running and... completed. I slammed the enter key again, but it did nothing this time since I hadn't entered a new prompt in the input field.

"You really need to work this out of your system, Rin."

I narrowed in on Caleb, forgetting about the program running. "You never call me Rin." Which was true. He hadn't, not since back when...

Leaning back in his chair and crossing his legs, Caleb rolled his eyes to the ceiling. "It worked just fine, didn't it?"

"Your cooling and the processing power are still not high enough. It hiccuped. A more accurate test would be to have *the proper specs...*"

"Let's run an experiment, shall we?"

Lifting my hands off the keyboard, I shoved it away. I swear it would have been much cooler had it not traveled less than an inch and instead knocked stay papers, folders, and pens off Caleb's desk like a good shove would on mine. "We just did!"

"This would be a different experiment. One where we see if you feel more emotionally stabilized after releasing your pent-up aggressions."

"I'm dating Cisco, Caleb! I'm not *releasing* anything around you!"

He smirked, even though he was still staring at the ceiling. "Tempting. You and I make a better match than you and Cisco. But I had different intentions. Check the bottom right drawer."

I slid the drawer open to find one squarish, squat crystal bottle filled with rich brown liquor. Knowing Caleb, it was a gift from his parents that cost more than my yearly salary.

Leveling his gaze on me, Caleb grinned an absolutely terrifying grin. Since I knew him, Caleb never grinned once, not like that. Finally, he said, "Let's share a drink, Rina."

Chapter Twenty-Six

Arcane magic

Mandy

I would never—ever—say my boss was a hot mess. Or absent-minded.

Never.

But Dr. Wellington walked with Cisco and me back to Cisco's office, allowed Cisco to get on the call, and then was ten minutes late to join the call with Cisco even though we were standing in the hallway outside Cisco's office and could hear Cisco plead for more sales pitches while Dr. Wellington reviewed my project details.

As soon as Dr. Wellington shamelessly ducked in, I was left alone in the hallway. I knew that once Wellington finished in there, Cisco and Rina would immediately head to Audra's for a family dinner. The dinner Rina considered—and failed—twisting my arm to get me to attend. She'd probably throw a second party if I showed up. Normally, I would have fought the social pressures my bestie's girlfriend put on me to ask Audra out and I would have, instead, pushed myself to go clubbing and found one poor decision after another to lament the next day.

But nothing felt normal since the whole car fiasco last weekend, or rather since I caught Cisco and—still shocked to say this at all—Rina scheming to fix my love life.

This hollowness followed me everywhere. Reminders of Mia and failure and what never seemed to be in my cards. It made my uselessness so utterly apparent.

As I trudged through the hallways, my ever-present, lonely specter kept shadowing me. I couldn't return to my empty apartment, yet the idea of going out and wallowing in fruity drinks with a stranger was equally unappealing.

I left work without Cisco's usual fanfare and drove around town, stopping at the first bookstore I saw. Something nagged at me when I reached for the handle. I'd heard about bookstores a lot—recently, in fact—last weekend...

Hand hovering over the door, I realized—*shit!*—Audra worked at a bookstore, but I struggled to remember if it was this particular one. Double shit.

No! *No dwelling on her*. Or anything. I released the door handle and meandered up the street without purpose, hoping something interesting would pop out and I'd drown myself in it. Forget what I was missing.

Another door called to me, and I opened it before I realized what shop I'd come to. The ringing bell shook me. And I saw comics and paintings on the wall... It was the comic shop. As in, the one Cisco dragged me to for his game.

"Hey, I'm actually closing early... oh." Arcane popped up, drumming his newly painted black nails on the protective glass top of his counter. "Mandy, right?"

Blinking, I tried to think of a way out. Something that didn't sound stupid or embarrassing because, obviously, whatever I said would get back to Mandy. Whoa! *Why did I care?* I wasn't going to ask her out!

Arcane stared at me, waiting for an answer. How long had I been standing there staring? "Y-yes." I didn't expect him to remember my name, which, in hindsight, was incredibly dumb. Why wouldn't he remember my name? I sat across from him for hours, struggling my way through the weirdest role-playing of my life.

"What brings you in?" he asked, still drumming the counter, though admittedly faster.

I pointed at the door. "I can go. You have to go soon. The celebration dinner and all..."

"You know about that?" Arcane leaned on the counter, sliding down, hands clasped but using his thumbs to massage his eyes. "It's going to be a nightmare. I hate bringing Brandon around *them*. Audra has it worse... our aunts, not just one but all of them, truly can't get it through their heads... but... you didn't come here for the Taylor family gossip."

"I'm—"

"Looking for something." Arcane jumped over the counter. "You just aren't sure what, right?"

How? How did he figure that out? Maybe his nickname wasn't too far off, and he held some magic no one else in the world had.

"You don't read comics, right?" Like a wizard or mentor from movies, he moved in and out of sight, walking the aisles. "Let's see. Something... down to Earth? Possibly speculative. I don't think you'd read anything too out there. Cisco seems into comics, but you... are you a novel reader?" He scrolled through books and comics as he asked.

My brain glitched. Eventually,—like an idiot—I nodded.

"I know when something weighs me down—" Arcane continued his slow looping around the store, searching the shelves for something specific. "—it can be difficult to decide what to read or even what to do next."

Ain't that the truth?

Oh, my God! Was it possible for me to leave? I mean, Arcane was being so nice. But he didn't need to when he had more important places to be.

I caught Arcane glancing my way. "I remember dating this guy, Steve, in high school. It was a pretty secret, under-the-radar kind of thing. But I was head over heels, so anything my friends said went in one ear and out the other. He was the boyfriend no one liked."

Oh, sure. I saw where this was going. Arcane seriously had his own psychic powers. Maybe he offered palm reading, and I missed the sign.

Arcane continued up an aisle, stopping occasionally to pluck a book or comic, then put it back instantly. I followed his progress but from the center aisle. "What happened?" I asked, curious if he'd parrot back what happened to me. Oooh! New theory! Maybe Arcane's magic was that he's been mirroring my life all along.

"I gave up theater for Steve. He didn't understand the value of arts like theater. He always said he hated other people gawking at me, 'laughing at me or making fun of me' and all that. But I gave up. I became what Steve wanted."

I didn't need this. I really should just leave. This was the most useless... wait... what? "Seriously?" I balked.

"Well, yeah," Arcane circled around to the other side of the store. "Teenagers rarely think they'll find someone who truly understands them. I couldn't let Steve go. Who else would *get* me?"

"But you have to stand up for yourself. People don't always like that either, and it might hurt like hell... and you might not find..."

"You mean find someone who will recognize your worth?" Arcane finished for me. "You're right, and it hurts like hell both to break up with someone or have your heart trampled when they walk away... but it's equally as hard to pick yourself up afterward. It took me way too long to realize I couldn't let the hurt define who I was. And I did, for a long time after Steve."

Stop it. Arcane smiled at me, triumphantly holding a book.

"Did you go back into theater?" I asked.

"I mean... come on." Arms open wide, he motioned to all the books, comics, and paintings on the wall, the dice, and the table in the back. "D&D? It's the perfect outlet for theater kids. Plus, I get to write."

"You wrote the adventure we played?" That made Cisco's starstruckedness more understandable.

"I've written... dozens of campaigns now, some short, some long. All fun, all with a purpose." Holding out the book, he grinned goofily. A lot like Cisco's brilliant smile that drew me to him when he started at Infinite Labs. "This should be a good one for you. I'm partial to more action adventure, but I have heard this light novel is amazing. Some delinquents squat in a general store... ah, I don't want to spoil it. Give it a read, though. If you don't like it, bring it back."

Despite having so many questions, I found myself drawn to the counter by an invisible force. God, I needed to know more. Like how Arcane moved past the hurt, how he was sure someone else would come along who wouldn't feel the same way, and how...

My phone's imitation piano chord struck with an incoming text.

Cisco: HELP! MAYDAY! SOS!!!!

"That seems bad." Arcane grimaced at my phone, which I'd set down on a picture of some superhero, rereading Cisco's all-capslock text freakout. Given how loud the words were, Arcane probably could have seen them from across the store.

"I'm sure it's not so bad," I said while I pulled my credit card out, then watched Arcane chew on his lip. "Cisco always exaggerates things," I assured him, "making mountains out of anthills all the time."

"That's not the phrase... never mind." Arcane's laugh resonated in my chest. So much like his cousin's laugh.

"I know." I laughed. "But I hated saying molehill when I don't know what one is. Anthills? I've seen plenty of anthills."

Sucking in his lips, Arcane clamped down, but laughter was not far off. "Fair enough."

Cisco's name appeared at the top of my phone. One text and we were already at panic calling?

Panic calls from Cisco died off in recent months. He'd definitely not done any since dating Rina. Steeling myself, I answered. "What could be wrong on a Friday night with your *girlfriend*, going to a party?" I chided Cisco as soon as the call connected.

"You need to come back to work. I can't explain... you just really need to see. And I need help."

Arcane dropped the book in a bag as if I was actually going to read it. But at this point, he had gone through all that work, and I couldn't let his kind gesture go to waste. Damn it! I wanted Arcane to dive deeper, not have to babysit Cisco's anxiety. "Why are you still at work?"

"I can't get Rina to leave yet." A struggle must have happened for the phone, and Rina's voice, came through the speaker, but I couldn't ask anything else before, "Correction, Rina shouldn't leave yet for the dinner."

In the background, Rina yelled, "And she never treated Audra like Audra was worth anything. Well, newsflash... Chelsea... OH! Did you know Chelsea's husband cheats on her?"

Eyes the size of his oversized dice on display, Arcane gasped, "Oh my God! Is Rina...?"

Cisco cheered. "Is that Arcane? Oh, yes! One or both of you. Please. Get down to Infinite now and help me! I can't take her to Audra's parents like this!"

Chapter Twenty-Seven

Applesauce is not the right word

Audra

Wes was supposed to be my saving grace. Rina always provided support, but she couldn't distract. Not like how Wes could divert conversations, channel his inner badass, and keep people like Aunt Chelsea happily at bay so well that they didn't even notice they were being steered away from their target.

But without Wes, there was no way to get through dinner, even with Mom bringing out unending amounts of appetizers, mystically making them appear from dark recesses like the bottom of the freezer. It was a valiant effort by Mom. All in vain, but valiant nonetheless.

The smile on Aunt Chelsea's face when she entered portended misfortune. It only took five seconds into our house, and her smile turned malicious towards me. Aunt Chelsea said, "Such a shame. I'd hoped you would take my advice."

Somehow, that was Chelsea's good mood. God, where was Wes? Because—arg!—that smile always spelled disaster. We're talking hours-long disaster. And with no relief from questions like:

"Are you even making minimum wage at the little bookshop?"

"Holes in your jeans are so unseemly. I don't care if it's a trend..."

"What good is an education... oh, my mistake, Audra, did you graduate from college? At least..."

"I'm not sure why you bother living with Wes and his roommate..."

The worst part is how much control did any of us have over Aunt Chelsea's tirades? Zero point zero percent control. That's how much.

"Chel," Dad cooed with some alcoholic drink at the ready.

NO! My body lay limp against the cough. Filling Chelsea with alcohol would make the situation worse, not better, Dad!!!!

Before I could try texting Wes, my stupid cousin read my mind and messaged:

> **Wes:** I'll be late. I'm coming. I swear. Sending Brandon ahead.

Brandon was literally as sweet as sweet could be. The absolute definition of sweet in the dictionary. But the poor guy put up with entirely too much crap, all while grinning his delightful, sunshiny grin. It bordered on criminal torture sending Brandon into this hellhole without Wes as backup.

However, now Wes' text had been nearly 45 minutes ago, and we were still in a holding pattern. Twenty minutes of Brandon trying to interject and utterly failing... I couldn't stand it any longer.

And since Rina was a no-show (entirely unlike her, and I'd have to get the details), I pleaded the next time Mom went by with cubed cheese and crackers, "Can we just start dinner? Wes will be fine coming in late and..."

"He's on his way!" Brandon jumped up. The rare enthusiasm caught everyone off guard. "I mean..."

Voices carried from the doorstep to us and the awkward silence that followed Brandon's outburst.

"I don't need help!"

That was Rina's voice! Oh, thank every freaking pastry and pastry god in existence. I would swear with pastries for an entire month if that were Rina!

Jumping up, I raced toward the door, but Rina beat me and threw it open of her own accord. On the porch behind her, Cisco, Wes, and Mandy stood staring like deer in headlights at my family. Wes? Oh no. Maybe his phone was acting up again. Brandon only just received his text...

"Perfect, everyone's here!" Rina pushed her glasses onto her forehead, wiped at her eyes, then complained, "What the heck? Everything's so blurry."

It should have been my first clue that something was wrong, but the spotlight was finally off me.

"No, no, no!!!" Cisco and Wes cried, both reaching for Rina too late.

She'd crossed the threshold and made a beeline for Aunt Chelsea, only pausing long enough to grab my arm and drag me along to stop directly in front of my aunt. "This is ludicrous. You people all ignore what is right in front of you."

"Stop her," Cisco mouthed.

Mandy's hand shot to her mouth before sliding up to the crown of her head. "Holy crap."

"Don't think I don't remember all the stupid innuendos you made. *Rina and Audra should 'just get married,'* as if it were a dumb joke. But you know what? I would be only so lucky to marry someone like

Audra! But even if I did, you—oh, you!—would ignore our love and what we were. A couple! Gah! I can't take how you forget how freaking incredible Audra is. And I'm talking about you, Chelsea! Plus, every time I'm around, I have to keep my mouth shut because no one wants to upset you, but I don't even know why they let your *fucking*—"

NO! Rina did *not* just swear! Out loud! I gasped so loud and so forcefully I choked. For as long as I have known Rina, this girl... this freaking girl...

"—toxic ass—"

Bless her heart. This right here was the exact reason I loved Rina Takata!

"—continue coming when all you throw around is the most harmful rhetoric known to man!" Rina finished, panting hard.

Aunt Chelsea's jaw dropped as she clutched at proverbial pearls. "What the hell is...?"

The entire world turned upside down. My blood turned to ice, leaving me unable to think, breathe, or do anything.

"Just shut up! It's because of people like you that Audra won't even try to date someone she likes because you can't handle the fact that she likes women! Well, newsflash, no one likes you! And I love Audra. She's my best friend!"

Out of absolutely nowhere, not even in my wildest dreams, did I expect Rina to kiss me. But she did! It was nothing more than a peck on the lips, but... daaaaaaamn. Between Mandy's unannounced arrival and the time since my last date—well, I battled chest butterflies already. The kiss rushed the butterflies to my head.

Rina, glasses still perched on her head, flushed cheeks, and near tears, cupped my face in her hands and gushed, "I love you! You deserve the best! And you should never listen to your stupid freaking extended family. I'm your family. And I say you do what makes you happy!"

"I don't understand what is happening," Aunt Chelsea stammered. "This is absolutely..."

"Beautiful," Mandy finished with a short round of applause.

The butterflies instantly multiplied and, like moths to a beacon, drew my gaze to Mandy.

Crushing me in a hug, Rina kind of collapsed in on herself and stole back my attention. I caught her, and that's when Cisco, bowing his way into the room with a mumbled introduction, helped pry Rina off me. "How much did she drink?" I whispered.

"I don't know. Caleb freaking gave her something he had hidden in his office."

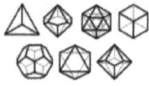

Mandy

Stomach flutters quickened as Audra blushed. Rina — our crazy, introverted, anxiety-ridden Rina — actually broke out of her shell and yelled what we all thought. Somehow, without reserve. God, I'd freaking tore down this bullshit before! What the hell was wrong with me that now, I couldn't even bring myself to tell a girl I liked her?

I assumed the woman fuming was none other than the famous Aunt Chelsea. Slowly, I took a breath and asked myself, what would I have done before? Before I hid the pain.

Arcane joined Brandon, smoothing his husband's suit jacket. Our eyes connected, and he gave his shoulders a shimmy.

It was as if it were that easy to just shake off the past.

Fine! I'd try.

"No one ever saw it coming." I joined everyone in the living room. "But Rina... she had a point, there."

A few of them.

A mirror in the hallway made me painfully aware of my hair (windswept and disheveled, no matter how many times I combed through with my fingers in the car) and heavy bags from days of fitful or no sleep. Plus, a long day at work—weren't they all long days? But Audra's hair sparkled with fresh bright pink highlights. Goodness, there was an audience, but I eked out, "You deserve the world."

Chelsea huffed, "You're all going to allow this utterly—" Though no one had been listening; Audra's parents gushed over Cisco and Rina, and Arcane drew Brandon close.

"Oh! Don't go on about ridiculous displays, Chelsea. We put up with too much of your bullshit as it is." I think it was Audra's mom who finally snapped. "You harp on my family all the time. If you can't keep your huge mouth shut, just get the hell out. Rina, dear... I'm making you some coffee."

Audra

Aunt Chelsea actually freaking listened and 'got the hell out,' though, with a bunch of yelling that no one listened to. Everyone became instantly concerned with Rina, who looked about ready to empty her stomach all over the living room.

Wes and Brandon sat Rina down while Cisco pleaded, "You've been going on like this for two hours. Just tell us: how much alcohol did Caleb give you?" He scooted closer, waiting for my mom to leave and finally brew the coffee before asking, "Bigger and better question: did Caleb drink with you, and is there security footage of anything insane he did? Because I cannot imagine this one bit..." Rina collapsed against Cisco, snuggling into his shoulder, green tinging her face.

When my mom returned with steaming coffee, Rina clutched the mug to her chest as if her life depended on it. Cisco brushed the hair out of her face, but it didn't help because when Rina tried taking a sip of coffee, she gagged on more stray hair. Plucking the glasses off the top of her head, Cisco tossed them to Brandon, who set them on the coffee table. Everyone made room to allow people to shift so that Cisco and Rina could sit on the loveseat (and make room for a massive bowl in case the inevitable happened).

Proper introductions started going around with Mom absolutely beaming while she shook Cisco's hand so violently that Rina moaned from the motion.

No eyes were on me or Mandy. Discreetly, I tapped her on the arm and pointed towards the kitchen. Damn her. Rina's wild courage was too contagious.

Mandy stood in the middle of our embarrassingly outdated craftsman kitchen, complete with deep wood accents that really muted the rest of our home's aesthetic.

I wedged myself in the counter's corner near the stove and reveled because I mostly stood upright and didn't collapse into a ball. "So, I am sure between Rina and Cisco, you know...?" If I said the rest out loud, my own vomit spree would put any I have seen Rina perform to shame.

"Yeah. I... I..." Holy crap. Mandy stuttered.

Were those... nerves? On Mandy?

Now or never. I could do this. *Just say the words, Taylor! GEES!*

I sucked in a long, shuddering breath and blurted out, "Look, I just need to say it, and if you say no, that's fine, but I guess if Rina can swear big time and say 'fuck' in front of my family—which I am reminding her of starting tomorrow until the day she dies—I can ask you on a date."

Mandy waited a long moment, then asked, "Was that you asking me out?"

"It was," I admitted, chewing on my lip mercilessly. And I will admit, it was a shameful attempt. "Will... you go to dinner with me? Not tonight's dinner...but... another dinner. Just you and me."

Mandy moved. Just a little move. She lifted the heel of her pump and tapped it on the laminate floor. "You should know," she started, sending my heart spiraling all the way into the basement. "I had a nasty breakup, well, a while ago, but I..." Both her hands ran through her hair, messing it up more.

I met her in the middle of the room. Pulling Mandy's hands back, I started combing out the most noticeable knots and replacing the hair so it lay flat. "Is that why all my awesome flirting went to waste? What tool would screw up with you?"

"I—" she stepped back. "—don't want to talk about it, and I don't want to hurt you."

Oh.

OH!

Holy crap. My heart slammed into my ribs. God, talk about the telltale heart being real and here in the Taylor household kitchen. Mandy had to have heard the hammering!

Breathe.

"We can go slow," I offered, praying to all the deities that I knew the names of because I felt her back away. Physically, Mandy took a step back. No, she was slipping away again. "And I will back off if you need me to and..."

"You're really sweet," Mandy sniffed with a distinct pre-cry warble.

There. It happened right through my fingers. Pain flashed in Mandy's eyes. "I can't promise I won't... I don't know... screw everything up." The longest pause ever. One where the entirety of a book could be read.

Finally, eventually, after the infinite number of heartbeats passed, Mandy said, "But, yes?" Mimicking me (or maybe Cisco), she tucked some hair behind my ear and said more firmly, "Yes."

The floodgate tore open.

Holy crap. HOLY CRAP!

Mandy said yes!

I think my jaw dropped because Mandy lifted my chin with her finger and then said, "If Rina can dive in, so can I."

Speaking of surprises Rina was capable of, I pressed closer. Mandy's smile infected me, bringing a giggle out. But she didn't back away. "Well?"

Mandy burst with a laugh and caught my cheek with a kiss.

"We could do better than a cheek kiss, right?" I asked.

"I'm a little out of practice..."

"So am I," I admitted.

Chapter Twenty-Eight
Bonus Epilogue

(Author's note: This was not in the original Kindle Vella Release)

Rina

"Are they out there?" Mandy asked from behind me and I jumped. Actually jumped. As in, my heels fell off and over and I stumbled.

Cisco caught me before I actually fell onto the stage where the audience of my peers—so, *so* many peers— could see me. His grin grew, and my mouth became an absolute desert. And then I squeaked. I needed to get used to his new haircut. Gone were the long, voluptuous waves that fell past his shoulders. Now, the waves were subdued, gelled back. Applesauce. My heart nearly leapt from my chest.

"It's going to be fine. Dr. Wellington is right in front. With Caleb. Just... present to them," Cisco said. "Ignore everyone else."

Mandy crowded behind me. "I see Audra. Just... explain it to her. Again." As soon as Mandy's grip tightened, I knew I wouldn't want to hear what was next. "Where did Caleb go?"

"I swear. Did he bring a flask? Because I cannot trust…" Cisco came nearer, arm hugging my waist. "No alcohol. Promise me."

"Rina?" Caleb's distinct coolness infected not only me but also Cisco and Mandy. Their arms gripped me harder. "Do you want to know who I saw in the audience?"

No! No, no, no, no, no! "Yes?"

From the stage, the conference chair took the microphone and said, "It is my warm pleasure to introduce this incredible team from Infinite Labs. I had the distinct honor of visiting their offices several weeks ago. This young team is making strides…"

Caleb got closer, repelling both Mandy and Cisco. They still held onto me and were going to take me off balance again, even without my shoes on. "Freddy…"

Nope! Not today! Good applesaucing grace. I was presenting my research! Mine! Well, they all helped but…

"Rina!" Cisco clamped onto my hand, dragging me from the light. How was I already in the light… but… "You need to wear your shoes!"

"You're a dangerous man," Mandy sighed. "Could you *not* make Rina embarrass herself?"

"What do I care if she's wearing shoes? As long as she's not falling over on stage and is able to present her research, I could care less."

Setting my shoes right with one hand so I could step into them, Cisco loosened his tie with the other. "Tell me you didn't spike her coffee?"

"I do not do anything non-consensual, Reyes. I've told you before, Rina agreed to the experiment. And fortunately for us all, it worked. I'm quite satisfied that our workplace is functioning normally again. Months without a major incident"

Cisco backed to me again, taking my hand. "Ready?" The introduction was winding down. Applause. Cisco kissed my fingers.

Mandy stared out at the front row. Next to Dr. Wellington, Audra had taken the day off work to come see our research presentation, but I knew what would be happening at dinner tonight. Cisco gave me a quiet *shhhh* and winked. "Time to shine," he beamed. "Or I take Lazy Beans Jr. hostage again."

"Freddy..." Caleb started.

"OOOOH!" I clomped on stage, my heels clacking loudly as the applause died down.

Also by

About the author

J.M. Guilfoyle is a mom of 3 who loves sci-fi, fantasy, anime, and K- & C-dramas. When not wrangling children, she can be found hiding in a corner with a mug of tea and her laptop, typing furiously and laughing at her own jokes, hoping not to be sucked back into the abyss of writing only fanfiction. Occasionally, she can be found writing short stories and posting them to her Substack blog.